LIFE LIST

PRAISE FOR *LIFE LIST:*
SELECTED SHORT FICTION

"Mimi Morton's prose is spare as the lives of the people she writes about. As they weave their way through these stories, we get to know them well — probably better than they would like. None of our business, they would say. But Morton makes it our business, and we care about them all, even (or especially) the most flawed."
-*Zeke Hecker, composer, lyricist, librettist, and essayist living in Guilford, VT*

"Set in a fictional, rural Vermont town, the stories both tell themselves and support each other, as a cast of common characters winds through. Most of the people we follow through these stories live at the margins: In old communes, or in a trailer with the rent in arrears. At any moment, several are homeless. Even an affluent gay couple becomes unexpectedly bankrupt. The matriarch of the collection is elderly Harriet Dawson, who resolutely lives 'Alone' with her dog, Blaster, resisting all attempts to move her into senior housing."
-*Don McLean, Vermont literary scholar*

"Treasure these wonderfully interlaced stories as I do. When these characters speak you hear authentic voices. These stories run on humorous, loving, political, sometimes stark dialogues where you will find your old struggling pals, your current friends in their troublesome quandaries, yourself, probably your parents, maybe even your grandparents, alive and carrying on."
-*Kathryn Kilgore, poet and writer*

LIFE LIST

Selected Short Fiction

MIMI MORTON

Burlington, Vermont

Copyright © 2021 by Mimi Morton

All rights reserved. No part of this book may be reproduced in any manner whatsoever without written permission except in the case of brief quotations embodied in critical articles and reviews.

ISBN 978-1-949066-68-5
Library of Congress Control Number: 2021906149

Onion River Press
191 Bank Street
Burlington, Vermont 05401
www.onionriverpress.com

To Kathryn Kilgore

Contents

Introduction ... 1

LIFE LIST

1. Life List ... 5
2. At the Foot of the Bed ... 10
3. The Borning Room Window ... 23
4. The Rectory ... 39
5. Pilgramage ... 47
6. A Castle in the Woods ... 56
7. Glory ... 72
8. Navigator ... 88
9. Cosmic Dust ... 95
10. Spring Snow ... 106
11. Alone ... 122

THE HYSTERICALS

12	The Cellar	135
13	Wild Mushrooms	150
14	Fire Wall	161
15	The Hutch	173
16	The Tenant	180
17	The Stern	184
18	Foxy	199
19	Flag Man	205
20	Corn Flakes	217
21	Pot Luck	226

About The Author   241

Introduction

Mimi Morton possessed a hard-won self-awareness, which she earned by being unsparing, fearless, and funny in describing her mistakes and transgressions while living in Montreal and southern Vermont. Because she was honest about herself to herself and others, she got better at living as she got older, and she applies that humble, humane honesty to many of her characters in these stories – the desire to become a better person, or at least to do the right thing once in a while. Mimi lived a full, vivid life and she remembered an uncanny amount of what she saw and heard along the way. Memories are a lush resource for the fiction writer, and her recollections served her well in creating a community of diverse characters, and their caustic and tender ways of talking to each other.

These stories are set in North Haven, a fictional Vermont town where proximity throws people together, as close neighbors, regardless of status, income, or social position. Drive along any road in town and you're likely to encounter a preening McMansion next to a marginal old dairy farm, followed by an 1810 federal, a well-kept double-wide, and a sagging hippie domicile. The people in these houses are not always friends, but they know whether they can count on each other for help, and their personal connections are often surprising, whether public or private. They are brought together in these connected stories, repeatedly in some cases. Their effects on each other – whether adjusting to radically changed circumstances, striving for virtue, or settling scores – are portrayed so realistically that we remember these encounters long after they occurred.

The book contains two collections of stories, in which many of the same characters reappear. The first section of *Life List* was written from 2009 – 2014. Mimi finished the second group of stories – *The Hystericals* – in 2020, as she was dying of cancer. She was determined to produce the book you are holding in your hands.

Rick Zamore, January 2021

LIfe List

I

Life List

I'll have a Grey Goose and a twist. I'm just back from France and now I gotta fly up to Vermont to deal with my mother. Let me tell you, France was way outside my comfort zone. I was doing it for my wife Lisa and her sister's kids. The girls are like our substitute daughters. Lisa can't carry a child to term. Very sad and we're not into adopting. Too many horror stories. I don't want to end up being sued by my kid, or knifed. Not that it couldn't happen with your biological kid.

Lisa has these books about French artists: so and so's garden, so and so's kitchen. The pictures are nice. Women like France. It inspires them and then they go crazy online. UPS has worn a rut through our pachysandra. The plates and the tablecloths and napkins. Anyway, Provence. She would like to go to Provence. Teeny little bottles of vinegar and olive oil that cost more than wine. When she was shopping for this stuff she was happy. Well, not unhappy. It took her mind off being pissed at me.

The pissed thing is many-faceted. The no-kid thing is part of it. My metabolism may be a factor. I'm way more hyper than she is. And sugar plays a role. I cannot get a buzz off M and M's. Which reminds me, hit me again.

I'm still not sure why Lisa married me. We were younger. I made her laugh and, I must face this, I felt differently about her than I do now. If I had to choose a word I'd say 'fascinated.' Honest to God, we'd be sitting watching TV and she'd cross her legs and start bobbing one foot in this little white thong sandal and I'd just stare at her ankle and the way she moved her foot so the arch would curve up and the gold polish on her toes. This is a woman with no negative body hair. I'd get down and try to locate follicles on her legs. None. She didn't have to say a word but she could do that, too. Talk about her weird uncle in Alaska who lives with some Indian. About what she bought. About her work. She teaches second grade and the kids *love* her. About what the neighbor's dog 'said' on his stupid blog. I would just enter another world. Lisa's World. And it was a hell of a lot better than Jimmy's World.

Then things changed the way they do. Like trees. You don't notice them growing taller until you go away and come back and WHAM! time has painted you a picture. I have had that experience. For instance when I was accused of cheating in my senior year of high school. Carl Corless, a kid with a glass eye was sneaking glances with his good eye over at my paper. I didn't rat on him and when our papers came up nearly identical I got nailed. I still feel good that I didn't rat. Corless was a jerk but he had a glass eye. I couldn't make him feel worse. "This will go in your record!" the asshole principal said. I graduated and never came back. I would go out of my way to avoid the place. But Lisa's sister sent her girls there. Megan went to a prom with a kid whose car broke and I was the only one available to pick them up at the gym so I had to break my own rule. I made myself a G&T, put it between my legs, drove down, and that's when I saw the trees. Freakin' fifty feet high pines. I almost puked it upset me so much. I do not like change.

Which is why things are weird now. Of course the nieces are changing, you can't avoid that. Jenn is majoring in psychology. I suppose she can make a living at it but I wouldn't want to spend my days with nut bars. Megan thinks she's going to be a golf pro. Just started golf camp. She's got better clubs than I do. Lisa took her for the clothes. Everything has to have a color theme. Hers' is Italy. Just try to find red white and green golf shoes. Lisa can do it.

And the other one, Jenn. If she wants to be a shrink (okay, a guidance counselor) why can't she find herself a boyfriend with a brain. She's a smart girl. We were told she tests very well. This guy—Boyfriend—is a parking valet. Can't find his ass with both hands. Okay, he parks cars at the only four- star restaurant in Baltimore. Maybe Jenn's lazy. In that she would be copying me.

Excuse me but I'm beginning to disgust myself. I need another drink. Vodka with buffalo grass? That's cool. My father was kicked by a horse when he was twelve. His dad had just died. The horse lived out back in a stable the way they had in towns then and he was feeding it one night and the thing kicks him, breaks his leg in two places and he gets taken to the hospital in the mail car of a train. The guy at the station gives him a pair of skates when he gets home to give him hope. I bet the blades were dull but he probably knew how to sharpen them, even as a kid. He made a knife sharpener for me. Still have it. Better than anything from Williams Sonoma. Kick me again with that buffalo.

No offense but I refused to have my one and only flight to Europe depart from Baltimore. So I hired a stretch limo and we drove up to JFK. I did not want to start a trip where I've had to go to get to every shitass convention of my life. Dallas. San Diego. LA. Atlanta. Phoenix was the worst. So what does my former employer Magna have lined up for the troops in Phoenix? A paintball bar. Guys are getting hammered and running around spattering each other with paint.

I remember one woman. Nancy Dooley from Duluth. Big with a mono eyebrow. The Chamber of Commerce up there would not be happy, but Nancy now represents Duluth for me. A lonely place where the women all look like Jackson Browne. She attached herself to me. Totally in the bag. I'd brought my binoculars so me and my buddy Wayne decide we'll go out birding. They call me Nature Channel. I always wanted to be a weatherman until I saw the science prerequisites.

I'm stoked to see a cactus wren, add it to my life list. Nancy Dooley wants to come. Great. It's a hundred and fifty degrees in the parking lot and she pukes on the fender of my buddy's PT Cruiser. So we dump her in the back seat with a bottle of water and get the air conditioner cranked up. Wayne stops for a six pack and Nancy wakes up and thinks we're abducting her. I start shitting bricks. I can see us handing in our real estate licenses, end of story. That's when I notice a cactus, right next to this phone booth and an old coke machine like something out of a movie. And on the cactus is this bird that I just *know* is a cactus wren. So I get Nancy looking at the wren and then she remembers. She wanted to go bird watching. A happy ending to a lousy Magna entertainment session. I'd like some more of that clear liquid.

You can see why I wanted to take off from JFK. Do something all the way right for a change. It was a hike up there but our driver Jerome understood acceleration. As we begin to roll, I look back at the house—the hedges and the tulip trees and the rose garden—and I think, "Wow! I wonder what Christmas would be like in that house?" And then I come out of it and realize, "*You* live in this house. *You* made this happen." All I want is to be out by the pool with my dad and a drink and I'm slow roasting a filet mignon the size of a newborn baby. Who the fuck needs France? But then Lisa leans over and gives me a kiss and says she loves me. Not a daily occurrence. And the girls say they love me and "thank you Uncle Jim for this trip." Something to look back on.

Okay, that's my flight, gotta go. You ever been to Vermont? Beards and bumper stickers. Right here has probably been the best part of the trip.

2

At the Foot of the Bed

In her dream, Harriet Dawson was her age now, 85, but she was pregnant. Then something woke her. A man was standing in the doorway. She screamed, struggled to untangle her legs from the bedclothes. A cramp seized her calf as she hoisted herself to a standing position. The back door slammed.

"Hell!" she yelled at the cramp. She hobbled to the window, clutched the sill and peered out into darkness. Were those footsteps thudding?

"Sick him, Blaster!" she hollered.

Where *was* Blaster, her black lab. She heard dog tags, felt his cold nose against her leg. She lowered herself onto a chair as her heart calmed down but now she was sweating. 3:00 on the clock radio. She felt a chill beginning, turned on the bedside lamp, pawed her bathrobe off the end of the bed. Blaster licked her hand. She picked up the phone.

"It's Harriet Dawson! On..." She had to think. No more RFD. "...three sixty-seven Sand Hill Road. Someone...a man was in my bedroom, woke me. Scared the daylights out of me..... Well, *good!* I'll be happy to see them!" She clattered the phone into its cradle, hand shaking. In all the years they'd lived here and now, since Tom's death, no one had broken in.

Lights in the driveway. She slid into her bedroom slippers and made her way downstairs, a hand on each rail, the cane around her wrist. In the kitchen, she felt for the light switch.

"Harriet, how you doin'?" Stevie Davis, a newly minted Statey, ducked in the doorway and removed his hat.

"Better now that you're here."

Stevie pulled out a kitchen chair and she sank down. She remembered when he used to come on Halloween with some sorry looking plastic costume from Vallerie's drug store and look at him now, a giant, and with all the gadgets on his uniform and with those wide-set Davis eyes. He set a glass of water in front of her.

"Quite a shock," she said, after she'd finished swallowing. "To be waked up out of a sound sleep by a strange man...." She coughed, rooted in the pocket of her bathrobe for a Kleenex.

"Tell me what happened." He opened a leather case, took out a pen.

"I just did! He waked me up, I hollered and he high-tailed it"

"So it was a male?"

"Isn't that who does this sort of thing?"

"Any unusual occurrences lately? People on the road? Phone calls?"

"Nothing. Very peaceful except on weekends when it's drunk

alley." Since the cops set up their sobriety check, people were using Sand Hill as a back way to town.

"We're working on that." He smiled.

"You have gorgeous teeth," she said. "Take care of them. You can't imagine how much you'll miss them when they start to go."

"Tell me about it!" he laughed. "These aren't real. Gran used to put Coke in our baby bottles. Do you lock up at night?"

"On occasion." Her son had lectured her about safety after her husband died.

"I'm just going to check around." Stevie disappeared into the living room. "The top panel of your storm door is cracked," he shouted.

"Happened before Tom died."

He reappeared. "Your front door is unlocked. "

"We never use that door," she explained. "I don't worry about locking when the weather's bad and it's been so wet lately." Why should he make her feel as if *she* was to blame?

Stevie raised his eyebrows. "Crime doesn't take a rain check."

"I really can't …. You're upsetting me."

"Okay," Stevie said softly. He picked up his hat. "I'll check out the dooryard. One of us'll pass by for the next few days. You need us, you call."

"That's very sweet of you." She could barely keep her eyes open.

No sooner was Stevie down the driveway than she snapped awake, creaked to her feet. In the dining room there was the tea service on the sideboard, the Waterford, those sterling pitchers she'd had a passion for that she used to fill with Tom's peonies. She sat down on the settee. How had the arms become threadbare? "What do I do all day but creep around and stare at things that I *used to use*," she said to Blaster.

A breeze wafted the dining room curtains. She shivered, struggled with the window, couldn't close it. In the living room, the grandfather clock ticked. Four AM. The windows here were closed and she caught a whiff of last winter's creosote from the wood stove and with it a rush of images. Tom with his avalanche of wood in the driveway. Jimmy, handsome and red cheeked, helping his father fill the woodshed. What would Tom have thought of someone in their bedroom? Inconceivable. *They know I'm alone.*

Why had he come upstairs? Nothing to take. Her jewelry box was stuffed with old campaign buttons and thread envelopes. But the house *looked* rich, a Federal that she and Tom had fixed up. They'd been happy to live quietly. But times were getting harder and the police blotter was full of break-ins. She sank down on Tom's old Lazy-Boy as a bird began peeping.

Barking. The grandfather clock had stopped at 7:00. She stood up and, joints snapping, made her way to the back door where Blaster was greeting Matt Lebow, the selectman.

"Dog doesn't have the sense that God gave geese." She grabbed Blaster's collar.

"*Ain't you a good dog!*" Matt scratched Blaster's ears. "Didn't mean to wake you. Just thought I should see how you was doin'."

Harriet squinted at the stove clock. "My Lord, it's nearly ten! I'll put the kettle on."

"Oh, nothin' for me." Matt rubbed his gut, eyed the cookie jar where a few of Harriet's hermits remained from her County Committee meeting.

She lifted the teakettle with both hands and set it on the stove. A headache was forming behind her eyes. "I thought it might have been one of those Shaws."

"New bunch in there now."

"Bunch...." Harriet mused as she poured Raisin Bran into a bowl. "Join me for breakfast?"

"Nah. Had something at the store." Matt accepted a cookie and slid it whole into his mouth. "Tina—that's one of them. Must be late twenties by now. My sister Alice was her para while she was in the grades. All them kids had trouble in school. I shouldn't talk. You got someone to fix that storm window?"

She'd forgotten.

"I'll stop back this afternoon and take measurements." He peered at the glass.

"You are a wonderful man!" Harriet waved goodbye and went back to her breakfast. She wouldn't hold her breath about that window. She was too old for ADT and for so much that people said would make her life easier, like the panic button she wore around her neck and had forgotten to hit last night. But first things first: finish breakfast, feed the dog, make the bed (she could not abide an unmade bed), get dressed, all this at her customary snail's pace.

As she pushed on with the day her mood improved, buoyed by minor victories. Bending to miter a corner of the bed sheet without twinges. Nearly touching a rose breasted grosbeak as she reached out the kitchen window to toss sunflower seeds on the bird feeder. Sniffing damp dish cloths as she pinned them to the clothes line on the back step. She loved to see a wash out, even the diminished ones of her widowhood.

She was finishing an egg salad sandwich when the phone rang. "Harry!" Her son Jim's pet name for her. "You okay?"

"I'm perfectly fine! How in the daylights did you hear about this?"

"About WHAT? What's going on? "

Harriet knew her son's nose for disaster. "There's really nothing—"

"Mom." His voice dropped. "What. Happened."

"I don't want—"

"I'm on my way to a closing. I don't have time to dick around."

"Dear, you're upsetting me." She held the receiver in both hands.

"Spit it out, Ma."

"Someone came into the house last night and woke. ..."

"So, you had a break-in." As if this wasn't what she'd said. "Look, I'm going through construction, I can't talk, I'll see you tomorrow."

"*What*?" Harriet bleated, but he had hung up. She'd been feeling absolutely fine and now her hands were shaking.

She struggled into Tom's old cardigan, found her cane and pocketbook and dug out her keys. She'd begun parking the car by the path to cut down on walking. She opened the back door for Blaster, then eased behind the wheel.

She drove down the Center Road, past the Grange, the Community Church, town office, the library, mowings, woods. She slowed as she approached a beat up ranch house surrounded by moldering prefab sheds, garbage cans, junk piles that tailed off into a weed patch bristling with iridescent whirlygigs, then more trash right up to the woods. A young woman in a pink sweatshirt stood outside the back door talking on a cell phone as a little boy dashed around the house and toward the road in pursuit of a cat. *That child!* Harriet jammed on the brakes and skidded into the ditch. A horn blared and a pickup swerved around her. Someone stuck a finger out the window as the driver gunned the motor and tires squealed. The woman glanced up, hollered at the boy, never taking the phone from her ear. Harriet gaped.

"What're *you* looking at?" the woman shouted.

Harriet fumbled for the window button. "I was afraid that child would run into the road."

"He's fine." The woman turned away and continued talking. "Old bitch nearly ran down Madison." Harriet saw a roll of tattooed flab below her sweatshirt.

She started the car. Wheels spun. Something... ... she hadn't seen the water. *Shit. Shit and carry two.* The Subaru stalled. She stared at the house: rotting sills covered with pink insulation board, tar paper. As she took in the view, calm settled over her. There was so much to see. An overturned gas grill. Dead televisions and kitchen appliances and discarded plastic toys. Near the woods, propped on its side, wasn't that a hot tub all twisted out of shape, as if by a pair of enormous paws? The woman and boy had disappeared. Now what? Harriet re-started the car and tapped the accelerator but no dice. She was stuck.

"I'll be right back," she told Blaster and edged out of the car. The back door had no step. She reached up and rapped with her cane. *What in daylights am I doing?* The young woman filled the doorway and Harriet was at eye level with a tattooed landscape of palm trees, ocean and mountains surrounding rhinestones erupting from the woman's navel, the crater of a volcano.

"Awfully sorry to bother you, I'm Harriet Dawson from out at—"

"Yeah, I know. Quigly's." Harriet was shocked to hear the name of her house's previous owner.

"I'm in the ditch—"

The woman strode to the car, slid into the front seat and with a few jolts back and forth drove the car to the side of the road.

"Thank you ever so much!" Harriet smiled with relief.

"No problem," the woman said, over her shoulder, as she walked back to the house.

As she pulled away, Harriet saw a face at a side window. She pressed the accelerator before she could think further.

The next morning was dry and mild, pie-making weather. She tried to open one of Tom's freezer containers. *blue Aug 06* was written in his uncertain penmanship. She broke a fingernail, cursed. Blueberries skittered over the counter and on to the floor. By the time she'd retrieved the broom from the laundry, Blaster was licking. She poured the remaining berries into a bowl, dragged the flour tin across the counter where she'd moved it now that she couldn't reach the upper shelves. Eventually she'd be leaving everything out on the counter, like old Millie Sturtevant down the road, sitting in the middle of chaos. Eventually? She was doing it right now, pushing sweepings behind the kitchen door, tossing her dirty laundry down the back stairs rather than carry the wash basket and then finding her underwear behind the telephone table. *Kim will take care of it,* she'd think, but by the time her housekeeper arrived Harriet would have forgotten about the floor sweepings or the missing panties.

She was rolling pie crust when the phone rang.

"How you doin'?" Matt Lebow. Why was it that people around here never identified themselves? "Your son was just by the office."

"Dear Lord it's not even noon!"

"He doesn't think much of our police work." Matt chuckled.

Harriet closed her eyes, then opened them to the sight of a white convertible pulling in the driveway. "I better finish making this pie."

She sprinkled flour on the cutting board and rolled out a bottom crust, coaxed the edge onto the rolling pin and unrolled it into the pie pan. Perfect. She dumped in the blueberries and a generous scoop of sugar, a squeeze of lemon juice and a sprinkle of cinnamon.

Her son entered the room as she was draping the top crust. He was in a business suit with his tie off. His curly fair hair seemed to have a reddish tinge. *Dye?* She would not inquire.

"Hello, darling. Just let me get this in the oven. What will you have for lunch?"

It was unlike her to continue what she was doing when Jim arrived, but on she went, crimping the edges of the crust between her thumb and forefinger, an activity that had always satisfied her.

"Had something at the airport." Jim kissed the air above her head as he described spare ribs by a Thai chef who grew five kinds of basil on his roof.

"That sounds lovely, dear." Harriet was trying to keep the oven open while she wobbled the pie plate onto the middle rack.

Jim was on the move, pacing from room to room.

"Nothing is missing, dear."

"No thanks to your cops. They all sound like they're a hundred years old. Why do you buy this stuff?" He held up a bottle from the liquor cabinet.

"Someone brought it to a party. We don't drink vodka."

"I'll buy you some Grey Goose Reserve." He opened the refrigerator, took out a beer, pulled the tab, gulped, belched, continued pacing.

She turned on the kettle, took out leftover tomato soup. Jim disappeared upstairs, came down in khakis and a tee-shirt.

She asked about the girls. Lisa and Jim's nieces were surrogate daughters to them. Harriet had grieved after each of Lisa's miscarriages and now they'd stopped trying. She didn't dare mention adoption.

"Megan's got a boyfriend so we haven't seen her as much. Guy hates me." Jim examined the door. "I'm gonna take a look outside." He peered at the broken storm window.

"That's old," she said. "Take Blaster with you."

"Hey, *buddy!*" Jim crouched over the dog, ruffling its ears. For a moment she saw him as the boy he had been, before he became a mystery.

When he'd gone out, she poured herself another cup of tea. No point in fretting about their differences. As Jim liked to tell her, she didn't live in the real world, the urban world of stress and threat and pollution.

"It absolutely *is* polluted here darling," she'd protested. "Have you taken a look at North Haven pond lately? All that weed from fertilizer runoff."

He'd rolled his eyes.

Jim came into the kitchen out of breath. "You got a problem."

He poured a handful of wood chips on the table. "You better come with me."

Harriet found her cane and followed him out to the road.

"See that?" Jim pointed to rectangular gouges in a telephone pole. The base of the pole was deep in wood chips where Blaster sniffed, lifted his leg. "Somebody's about to sabotage your line. The dog's on their scent."

Harriet guffawed in relief. "That's nothing but a pileated woodpecker hole. A real nuisance for the power company. You don't have pileateds around Baltimore?"

"Well, fuck me!" Jim's face went deeper red.

That night she was kept awake with a ferocious case of heartburn. Jim grilled steaks with béarnaise sauce. Red wine had never agreed with her but she drank a glass. She wanted to hear about his trip to France but they never got beyond restaurants and were interrupted by his phone. He'd just closed on a showplace for an IMF vice president. Jim quoted many thousands of square feet. Maids' quarters, guard house, squash and tennis courts. He swore her to secrecy. *Why?* She was too tired to ask. Tired but she tried to be proud. He'd wanted to go with Sotheby's and the new job, a month after Tom died, had brightened that bleak time.

She lay thinking about Jim's house outside of Baltimore. The great room with chandeliers and palladium windows. The unidentifiable steel appliances in a kitchen as antiseptic as a morgue. The automatic cleaning system that connected with a frightening network of ducts in a cellar with a game room, sauna, wine cellar and storage rooms containing wheeled racks for the overflow of their clothing. And if this was Jim's lowly basement, what must the IMF lord's basement be?

He was standing at the foot of her bed. She stifled a scream.

"Something's going on outside," Jim said. "Don't get up."

She obediently lay back down. His flat tone did not reassure her.

"Don't shoot!" A voice outdoors.

She staggered to the window. Moonlight revealed Jim in the front yard holding…could it be Tom's woodchuck rifle? A figure in the road was backing away, beginning to run.

"Jim."

He looked up, turned back to the road.

"Dear, please come in."

"What are people doing in your field?"

Oh, for the Lord's sake. "Probably looking for nightcrawlers. It's the time of year."

"*Nightcrawlers?*" As if she'd said 'extraterrestrials.'

She made her way down the front staircase and he came inside. In the light of the front hallway she could see he was sweating.

"Really, dear. There is nothing to worry about."

Jim replaced the rifle by the cellar door.

"It's all right, dear, really it is."

"I doubt that, Mother." The name shocked her.

He was looking at his phone. "You should NOT be living out here." He tapped the screen. "I'm on the record as having expressed my concern. "

Whose record? What record? Harriet slowly mounted the stairs, then turned and looked down at her son where he stood peering at his phone. A wall sconce picked out the red tint in his hair. *My poor baby.*

"Before you leave tomorrow, perhaps we could look for that pileated woodpecker." Even as she spoke, she knew she was wrong.

"Don't change the subject, Harriet." He looked up from the screen. "Stuff is going to happen."

3

The Borning Room Window

Matt squatted on Harriet Dawson's front step with his tape measure. A few weeks earlier, Harriet had called him from hip rehab, asked him to build her a ramp up to her front door. She'd probably be coming home before the holidays so he needed to get busy. She wanted it to match the stone steps. He had to laugh when he thought of the cost of granite and how in hell he'd transport it, let alone the problem of supporting a twelve foot long slab with a two foot rise and making it flush with a pine threshold. The weight of the stone would likely throw the door jamb even further out of plumb and put added stress on the rotting sills, causing the crisis to move down the line as corner posts shifted, beams sagged, plaster cracked. He'd seen old houses ruined by some handyman's good intentions. Matt did not want to be that man. He told Harriet she'd love the price of pressure-treated southern yellow pine.

Ringing in his pocket. He dug out his phone.

"Matthew?" he recognized Yvonne Sykes who ran the lunch counter at the country store. She was the only female who called him by his full name, her way of reminding him of their time of closeness long ago. She'd done a fair bit more than hold his hand while he was going through his second divorce.

"There's a lady here says she's been trying to reach you." Rustling as Yvonne transferred the phone.

"Is this Matt Le-BOW?" An out-of-town voice.

"It is." He felt a pinprick of foreboding.

"This is Brook Calder."

Sounded like a celebrity's name. She wondered if she could meet him. It wasn't a story for the phone but she had something she needed to discuss.

"Long as you ain't tryin' to sell me something!" Matt let out a bark of laughter.

He'd come down to the store, he could use another coffee anyway, but she hesitated. Could she talk to him somewhere quieter? Matt gave her directions to Harriet's house.

He lit a cigarette and walked around the house surveying last year's paint job. You couldn't slap just one coat of paint on these old wooden clapboards and expect it to last. Waste of his time and Harriet's money but it was all she wanted. "I don't know how much longer I'll be here," she said. Long enough to see her pantry window rot out because she wouldn't buy a custom storm. "I like it just as it is, ancient," was her defense. "A rare borning room window." Matt didn't want to burst her bubble by telling her he'd cut the space for that window himself before Harriet had ever seen or heard of the house.

Matt had been born in North Haven and lived there all his life, except for three years in the Navy, stationed in Hawaii. He knew the lineage of most of the town's old houses and cellar holes. He remembered where springs rose and where barns had burned or collapsed. He could tell you where the remaining outhouses were moldering and who still preferred using them to what they had indoors. He could sense where to get perc because he was an occasional dowser, taught by his former neighbor, Russell Cates. He didn't provide advice unless asked, so he just watched as newcomers spent thousands drilling through rock to get water they might have found easily and cheaply within sight of their money pit.

He was related to the landscape. He knew past and present sugar bushes, wood lots and deeryards. He could find lady slippers and trailing arbutus in spring and bottle gentians in September. Now that there was an interest in that sort of thing, he could be persuaded to lead birders to barred owl trees on a moonlit night. If, during drought, a moose stumbled into town, Matt was one of the first to see signs of it.

He'd visited, eaten in, got drunk in, gotten thrown out of many houses in North Haven but he'd lived in only three: the cape on Old Tavern Road where he'd grown up; the trailer on the home property where he and his first wife had lived; and the house he lived in now, a log cabin kit house behind North Haven Pond that he and Trish, his second wife, had built after their son was born.

If you'd worked in and around North Haven all your life it

wasn't unusual to become involved in its governance as long as you didn't talk politics. Matt was affable with a good disposition. "You're kinda like a beer-drinking Buddhist," Yvonne Sykes said. "No bad thoughts."

He couldn't include his two ex-wives among his fans, but he held nothing against them. The first marriage, right out of high school, was interrupted by the service. When he got home his wife announced that she needed to leave in order to *find herself*, as she put it, which was okay with him, he was still in his twenties. His second marriage ended after his son Danny died crashing a vintage Mustang that Matt had helped him fix up. Booze was a factor and Matt's wife Trish never stopped blaming Matt for his own drinking. Within a year she'd met somebody else and moved to Florida. The following winter, after a blizzard, the town plow inadvertently smashed the cross that Danny's friends had planted at the crash site. Matt found bits of wood and plastic flowers in the ditch the next spring. He was relieved not to have to see the cross every day on his way to the town office.

Matt believed that there was nothing you couldn't forget or, in the case of his son's death, endure. He was able to distance himself from the grief that had caused his son's mother to switch husbands and states. Stay put, keep busy, be friendly was Matt's solution to tragedy. He recognized so many cars around town that he'd stopped waving, just raised a finger off the steering wheel in greeting as he passed. The scanner was rarely silent and life remained a gamble, which was why Matt played the lottery every Friday for the fourteen years since Danny's funeral and gave his winnings to the town, earmarked for whatever projects needed funding, mostly roads and the school.

He pissed on the well head and was just zipping up when he heard leaves crunching. Harriet's son had taken her dog down south or Blaster would've been barking. A new SUV pulled up behind his truck and a woman got out. Tall, long dark hair. Black outfit. High boots. Long coat. She stood with the door open, motionless, looking around like a deer at the edge of a clearing.

Matt stared. *My gawd you're good-looking.*

She came toward him, not smiling, eyes narrowing almost to a squint. He was fine print she needed to read. Was she his height, or was it her tall black boots?

"Matt Lebow?" This time she pronounced it right.

"Yep." Matt saw her nervousness and her age. What was she, 40? Women around here just didn't look this good ever. True fact of rural life.

"Brook Calder." She held out her hand.

Matt stomped on his cigarette, gripped her icy fingers and shook.

"I think you knew my mother, Lynn Calder."

At first a blank, and then curtains, waves, hills parting and time's pinball back-rolling until CLINK!

"Oh dear lord it's been donkey's years, I wasn't out of high school." He felt for his pack of Camels.

"She died last month." The woman glanced down and her hair fell across her face. She brushed it back and looked up. "She asked me to find you so we could discuss something."

Matt felt his heart speed up. "You're getting me discombobulated." He took out a cigarette, put it away.

"Could we go where it's warmer? I didn't bring the right clothes." She glanced at the house.

"I don't have the key. Just working outside here. You want to go for coffee?" Matt glanced at his watch. Nearly 5. She could follow him to the Vegas.

He got in his truck and lit a cigarette. He hadn't had a drink since Danny died and today would be no different. The Vegas across the river was a place he'd be unlikely to see an old drinking pal or at least anybody with the brain cells to remember him.

As he led the way down River Road and across the bridge, he did the math: if he'd known her mother when he was 16 and her mother had been how old then? Nearly 30? That would put her mom in her 70s? Jeezum crow.

He'd never heard anything else about Lynn after that winter he showed up one night at Fern Hill, as the commune was called, in what was now Harriet Dawson's house. Dear Lord! Here was this girl standing outside the house where her mother had spent time and he hadn't had wit enough to point out the coincidence.

Counter stools at the Vegas Diner were filling up and Matt was relieved to see he recognized no one. He steered Brook to a booth.

"What can I get for you people this evening?" A waitress Matt didn't recognize looked old enough to retire but probably couldn't afford to.

"A Heineken," Brook said.

Matt ordered a coffee. He could tolerate being around booze just like he could withstand a selectboard meeting where some asshole stood in the back challenging him on the budget numbers. You don't let the bastard get close to you. Alcohol had taken his dearly beloved son and now he kept it at a distance. Being in the Vegas was bringing him closer than he wanted to get to the bastard's lousy breath but he'd been too spooked to think of an alternative.

"So, I'm going to cut to the chase." Brook steepled her fingers. Matt stared at gold rings. Nothing on her wedding finger. "My mother was a single parent. She'd always told me she got pregnant from a one-night stand; she moved on and never knew his last name."

Matt felt his bowels lurch.

"But when she found out she was sick, she changed the story."

"What are you telling me?"

They stared at each other.

"Just before she died, she gave me this." Brook took out her wallet and handed Matt a social security card. Lynn Lee Calder in black letters. Along the soiled edge of the card was printed in pen: Matt Lebow.

"Was she sure?"

Brook rolled her eyes and for an instant Matt saw a much younger woman.

"I'm not prepared to speculate. She was lucid. She wrote your name right in front of me."

Matt turned the card over and laid it on the table. How could he connect to something he felt no relation to? He picked up the card and handed it back to her.

"So what do—" He caught himself and rephrased. "What can I do for you?"

She pinched the skin between her eyes. "Excuse me. I'm a bit tired. Too much traveling." She took out a pair of wire-rimmed glasses. "Helps with jet lag." The glasses made her look like an actress Matt had seen in a spy movie.

"She wanted me to find out about your genetic history in case there were any health issues that could affect me. She had a lot of regrets."

"Regrets." Matt was only half listening. *This woman is my daughter.*

"Being a single parent. Her career was everything. She didn't take care of me and she didn't take care of herself. She sacrificed everything for her work. It was not an easy life and the strain caught up with her."

Matt cleared his throat, searched the room for a place to stash his gaze. Antique New Hampshire license plates were nailed to the wall. *Live Free or Die.* The motto's absolutism impressed him when he was young but over the years the words lost their punch, or he had. He stared at a wide suspendered back at the counter. The man glanced over his shoulder and Matt looked away.

"That's why I'm here," Brook said. "I told my mother I'd find you and check your health background."

"Health," Matt repeated. That's all she wanted? "Nothing unusual comes to mind. Be better if I stopped smoking and ate less. All I take is blood pressure pills. Runs in the family."

"Could I have a copy of any medical records? You could fax them?" She sounded worn out.

"I don't know as anybody has much on the family. Don't know how these outfits organize. Privacy laws might be a problem ...." He trailed off. What could he do? He tried to steer clear of doctors and hospitals.

She took out her cell phone and stared at the screen, put it back in her purse.

"Heart, stroke," he went on. "Carried off my grandparents. Dad had diabetes so I guess that's something. My mother gained too much weight, broke her hip and sorta faded out. Just your garden variety of ailments."

Ringing. She picked up her cell.

"'Excuse me but I need to take this. I'll be right back."

When she went out to the parking lot for better reception, he was glad to have a moment alone. That he didn't have a clear memory of her mother made him uneasy. He recalled long dark hair and long legs but he couldn't bring back her face. Nice eyes; he decided she must have had that. Mostly he remembered someone who had stepped from another world where people used words differently and were moving on, toward what he couldn't imagine. She was so much older. But what the two of them said or did, even the sex, was gone. He did remember that it was the first sex he'd had in a bed rather than the back seat of a car or a couch. The first woman he'd seen completely unclothed. By late summer she was gone. He began his senior year feeling detached from his friends until he grew lonely and settled back into the life he'd known. Lynn made a good story. He must have bragged about her but he couldn't remember that either.

"Everything okay?" he asked, when Brook returned, a routine question he'd ask a friend who was interrupted by a call but, of course, she wasn't exactly his friend.

She nodded, tapped the screen and put it down. They were silent, staring out the window at the river where the resident Canada geese floated in the dusk.

"This is weird," he said.

"No kidding," she said.

At that moment he decided he liked her and a memory surfaced. "At night, I'd take her out back and show her the constellations. One sunset, we walked in the woods and flushed a big buck. She loved that."

"Really." Brook raised her eyebrows. "I never knew she cared anything about nature. When I was a kid it was a big deal if she took me to a zoo. That was my idea of nature. She was just totally focused on her work."

"Work."

"Public policy. Families and children. We moved all over. It was difficult for women to get tenure at that point but finally she did. Columbia. She did a lot of international consulting."

"You must have been proud of your mother." When she did not reply, he went on. "Do you have any...." He searched for a neutral word. "Siblings?"

Brook gave a short laugh. "She could barely manage with one." She yawned. "Excuse me. And you? Do you have children?"

"A son." Matt looked out the window but was stopped by his own reflection and the row of bodies on the bar stools. It was full dark. "My son passed away." And then, because he felt he had to explain, "Car crash."

"I'm sorry," she said.

You don't know anything about it. Then to make up for his bitterness, he began a story. "The night I met your mother I'd come up there to plow somebody out so's they could catch the bus to New York the next morning, although I doubt one would have been running, the roads were such a mess, but that's another story. I had my dad's old Dodge dump truck with the plow on. I wasn't legal, neither was the truck."

Brook was looking out the window. Bored?

"Everyone was running around buck naked."

That got her attention.

"There'd been a storm- but they had power; the house was all lit up, with music blasting. I finished moving snow as best I could and was about to leave but I was young and curious, plus I was hoping to get paid on the spot, so I went up to the door and I'll never forget, a girl comes out in a bathrobe. 'I'm your genial hostess,' she says. I'd never heard anybody talk like that."

Brook took out her cell phone and fiddled with something, then laid it between them. "I hope you don't mind if I record this. I'm so exhausted right now that I don't trust myself to remember what you're saying. I can listen when I get home."

"Home."

"Berlin."

"Germany?" He stared at her.

She nodded. "So, you're in that house with the naked people."

"First let's order something. My stomach's rumbling so I can't hear myself talk."

Matt signaled the waitress and asked for a cheeseburger and fries. "And the same thing for her." Brook began to protest but Matt held up his hand.

"Somebody made a sauna in there," Matt continued. "Just a pot bellied stove with rocks on top and a bucket of water. I'm standing out there in the mudroom which was, let me tell you, *cold,* and the door to the sauna opens and a cloud of steam rolls out and I look down and there's a pile of naked people rolling around. Reminded me of a bunch of snakes I'd found under our refrigerator, copulating. My mom made me sweep them out the back door with a broom."

"That's quite an image."

"I doubt people were having sex although that might've been my impression when I first saw those naked bodies. You have to remember I was just a farm boy."

The waitress returned with a plate of French fries.

"These are hot so I wanted to get them right over to you."

Brook glanced at the plate dubiously. Matt pawed up a clutch of fries and ate hungrily.

"This place is better than I remember," he said with his mouth full.

"So that's when you met my mother. In the sauna."

Matt wiped his mouth. "I don't remember her in the sauna *per se*. "He liked the sound of that phrase; he'd heard it but never used it. "She showed up later in the kitchen. I do recall her words to me, 'Where did you get those shoulders?'"

Brook looked at his shoulders.

"I was big for my age and I'd done a lot of work around home."

"So she liked your shoulders."

"It would seem so. You know, there was a lot of partying at that house and after the first night I just found my way back there."

"How often?"

"Oh, maybe a half dozen times after that first night. Then she went back out west—Chicago?"

Brooked looked at her untouched plate. "I'm trying to get this in perspective."

"Yeah well it was the times. Parties...hippies...you know...."

"She wasn't a hippie." Her expression—unsmiling, assessing. She considered him responsible for wrongdoing: he became her father.

"Neither was I. No hippie."

As if to settle the issue of what he was or was not, she picked up her phone and pointed it at him.

"You don't need a picture of an old gink like me."

"Right now, I don't know what I might need, "she said. "This is just as bizarre for me as it is for you. I never even fantasized about finding my biological father."

"Sperm donor," Matt heard himself say.

"She wasn't looking to get pregnant!" Brook glared at him, then her look dissolved. "There were times when I wondered why she kept me." She took out a Kleenex. "Excuse me." She blew her nose. "I don't mean that to sound melodramatic but she wasn't particularly maternal."

"I'm sorry it was like that for you." Matt reached across the table and put his hand on top of her hand. "Nobody deserves......" he shifted gears. "Everyone needs... ..." He let it go. Under her hand was the cell and he felt it vibrate. He slid his hand off her hand as she picked up the phone.

"It's not important." She put the cell down, took off her glasses and wiped her eyes. When she replaced her glasses, her manner changed.

"Here's my contact information." She passed a card across the table.

He read her name, a German street name and a long string of numbers. He recognized an English word.

"You work in a bank?"

"Investment. Yes." She picked up her phone, tapped it, put it in her purse. "Give me your email."

All business, just like her mother. Matt drained his coffee mug.

"Don't have email. You'd have to go through the town office and they wouldn't appreciate that. I'll call the hospital and see what they can do."

She glanced at her watch. "I have an early flight tomorrow and I have to get this car back to the city." She picked up her scarf.

What in the hell was going on? Matt was still trying to figure out who this woman was.

"You're not going to drive all the way down there now!" He stood up as she slid out of the booth. "Don't you want to see the house where your mother lived? Fact is, you've seen it. You met me there." He was following her to the cashier. "I could show you the window I cut in your mother's room." She gave her credit card to the waitress.

"Please let me do this," she said over Matt's protest. A man glanced over from the counter as Matt put his wallet away.

"I'm going to finish this story or die trying," Matt said, out in the parking lot. An icy wind blew off the river. "Your mom was sleeping in the old store room. No window, stuffy as hell. So I brought my chain saw over and cut her a window. It's there to this day and everyone thinks it's original to that old house."

Brook smiled. Was she indulging him? A few minutes before she'd been crying. "I'd like to see it, I really would. I'm sorry about the rush. If I'd been able to find your number, I could have given you some advance warning and we might have had more time but, as it is...." There was that reproving glance again. *He* was the reason she didn't have time to stay. Was this banker's logic?

"It may not seem like much but we've accomplished what my mother wanted. Closure. That's how I understand her asking me to find you."

"What's being closed?" Matt shouted at her back as she ducked into the car. This young woman had torn something open in his head and he was going to have one hell of a time making things the same as they were before she phoned.

She lowered the window, looked up at him. Her glasses glinted in the floodlight.

"So, what you want is a sheet of numbers or statistics, some *print-out*," he continued. "You don't want to know *me*."

"This is what Lynn wanted," she said. "I don't know what I want."

On the way home, Matt was so lost in thought that a car had to blink its lights before he remembered to lower his high beams. "I'm part of what made you," he shouted at an imaginary Brook. "Why'd she name you what she did? Maybe because the two of us walked up a brook one day." Another detail he forgot to tell her. "Years from now you'll figure that you want more from me and you'll come back but it just might be too late."

Near the crash site, he pulled over, stopped, turned on his hazard blinkers. He'd been too late to see his son taken from the car, had passed the ambulance, turned around, followed it to the hospital, the worst ride of his life. Now he put his head down on the steering wheel. "Oh, my boy," he sobbed. "My only one."

Eventually he blew his nose, turned off his blinkers and drove on. Yvonne Sykes' car was outside the country store. He stopped.

Yvonne looked up from the register. "So, who is she?"

Matt stood in the doorway uncertainly.

"Oh, my gawd, what did she do to you?" Yvonne came toward him. "Sit down and tell me the sad story."

4

The Rectory

Harriet was returning from drive-by confession, something Father Marc had begun in the warmer months to attract younger parishioners too busy to park and come inside the church. As far as Harriet could see, the line-up was oldsters who wanted to avoid walking. A circular driveway led past the rectory's concrete front porch where Father Marc sat in a lawn chair with a plastic water bottle. The rectory. What an eyesore! A grey stone veneer split level with not one scrap of landscaping. Confess, receive penance, and go, presumably, while praying.

She knew these were desperate times for the church but Harriet wanted more bang for her buck. She liked a priest to be sequestered behind lattice in a dim atmosphere conducive to the admission of sin. As a child, she'd thrilled at the shadowy vastness of the Baltimore cathedral as she stood beneath its vaulted nave. Now here she was leaning out the car window in full sunshine, gassing with a soft-featured young man in a black sports shirt and hair that stood up in greased tufts. Today all she could dredge up was an apology for missing mass the past two weeks. Her allergies were a fib. She'd been exhausted by her son Jim's recent visit and what had prompted it—that break-in. Or had it just been her nightmare? She might never know.

"Three Hail Marys and three Our Fathers and you're good to go!" Father Marc smacked a black fly on his neck.

"Thank you, Father," Harriet laughed. "But I honestly don't see the point of all this at my age."

"What we don't see has a habit of tapping us on the shoulder." Father Marc patted his own shoulder.

Teach your grandmother to suck eggs, Harriet thought, as she waited to pull into the street. She heard a child's cries and her stomach tightened. Along the sidewalk came a woman pushing a baby in a pram with a wailing toddler by her side. She appeared to ignore the little boy as she pulled him along. He cried harder, tried to shake off her hand. She stopped, squatted in front him, scolding. He shrieked, eyes closed, face crimson. His mother gripped his shoulders and shook him. The child's head wobbled back and forth in a horrible parody of assent. Harriet could watch no more and she pressed the accelerator. Thankfully, no cars were approaching. "No, never, no, no," she whispered as she drove on, gripped in the claws of memory.

When she pulled into her own dooryard, she was relieved to see her housekeeper Kim standing by her truck smoking like a truant.

"Hey, I hope I didn't surprise you." Kim smiled as if a joke was on Harriet. "Bill's got the kids at his mom's so I thought I'd give you an hour."

Kim's cleaning was erratic but Harriet appreciated her companionship as much as she needed her to turn the mattress and wash windows.

"And how are things with you?" She tried to sound breezy, not like the basket case she felt herself to be.

"We got Chad with us now." Kim rolled her eyes. "Last Thursday I come home and he's sittin' on the front step lighting matches. So I'm standing in front of him with my arms full of groceries and he's droppin' matches, makin' a mess on my new slate. I go, 'What're you doin?' He's like, 'Nothin.' I go, 'No you're not, you're wastin' my matches. I need those for the wood stove.' He's like, 'How ya know they're your matches?'" Kim lowered her head, glared at Harriet through her eyebrows. "Chad has stolen from *every member* of my family."

Kim piled on details of her brother-in-law's offenses but Harriet was oblivious, still hearing the toddler's cries, seeing the mother's rage. She watched absently as Kim wiped down her bottle collection on the windowsill, waved a Swiffer over the bookshelves.

"He stole a case of Bud out of Billy's truck and when Bill asked him for the receipt Chad said he spit his gum in it. *Chad would never be that neat.*" Kim laughed and Harriet smiled weakly. *Play along*, she thought. *Keep her talking.*

"So how did you end up housing Chad?"

"Lost his license. Again." Kim raised her eyes to the ceiling. "Not that it matters 'cause his truck is dead. And no place to stay since Tina kicked him out. So we said he could have the walk-in closet off the kitchen. That was before he drank all Billy's beer. Now he's living out back under the picnic table." Kim's laughter broke up into coughing.

Harriet followed her into the living room where Kim was replacing air fresheners. "I should make lunch. Are you hungry?"

"Nah," Kim polished the trim on the fireplace screen. "I got a Pepsi around here someplace."

She was picking at egg salad when Kim appeared in the doorway.

"You got six of these jammin' the drawer in your side table." She held up glass votive cups.

"Pitch 'em!"

"Really?" Kim raises her eyebrows. "There's candles, too."

"Yours."

Kim smiled and, not for the first time, Harriet saw her beauty. "I always say you could be living in a cardboard box on the street, but if you smooth out your blankets, light a couple of candles, you can feel pretty damned good."

How I wish I believed that, Harriet thought. "Say! Take that snifter!"

Kim's face changed. "No, really? This is neat." She held the crystal goblet to the light. "You don't want to get rid of this."

"Yes, I do." Harriet felt a jolt of energy spin in the top of her head. "And I want you to get rid of that man or he'll keep robbing you blind. Set limits! Don't let people take advantage of you."

"It's not like I can wave a magic wand!" Kim made an arc with the Swiffer. "I got Bill and all his crap. I got the kids. Chad's their uncle." She disappeared upstairs and Harriet heard the groan of the vacuum cleaner.

She walked out on the porch with Blaster at her heels. The day had transformed and was now dry and clear. She watched the dog writhe on his back in the grass, then stand up and shake himself and stretch out with his belly to the sun. She looked out at the beauty of the day and felt only sadness. In a corner of the porch stood her son's old tripod and scope in its plastic shroud. Harriet uncovered it, dragged over her chair. She put her eye to the binocular and tried to focus. Gradually, a scene sharpened. Ah... a swallowtail butterfly drifted across her view, rested on a peony. A phoebe launched itself and SNAP! grabbed an insect out of the air, swooped back to its perch. She swiveled the scope downward into a blur of greens, focused in on a wasp and a—what was that? A yellow jacket? The insects battled, tumbled out of sight behind an iris sheath. "My sweet boy," she whispered. "No, no, no."

She forced her eye back to the scope. An emerald oval moved on a leaf. Could there be such an insect? And why so beautiful? She herself had chosen not to remember a great many events, people. *Just put them out of your mind* and she imagined the moment fading, the person floating away to a mental limbo.

"You crack me up, you really do." Kim stood in the doorway. "Out here lookin' at your bugs."

Startled, Harriet pulled away from the scope. She followed as Kim carried a cardboard box with the votives and goblet to her truck.

"I hope I didn't overstep by talking about Chad," Harriet said.

"You deserve some respect. And you can be an example to your girls by setting limits with him."

"Yeah?" Kim cocked a half smile. "We'll see."

With a rising sense of panic, Harriet watched Kim's truck as it swung into the road, back-fired, accelerated. As crazy as the thought was, she wished she could trade places with Kim heart and soul. She took her cane and walked across the grass to her shade garden and tried to admire violet periwinkles, white trillium fading to pink and, whitest of all, her blood roots. Then she returned to the porch and sat in the midst of the high insect sibilance.

She tried to focus the binocular but soon replaced the plastic cover. Somewhere an ambulance screamed and her stomach tightened. She couldn't banish the sound of that toddler so like her son at that age. The sturdy little body, the curly red gold hair and fierce blue eyes and especially the incident of the shirt. They were going to a birthday party. It was a hot afternoon and she laid out a new short-sleeved shirt but he wanted his flannel cowboy shirt. She had insisted and he had raged, beating his head against the French door until a pane cracked. You had to educate a child about limits and authority. He couldn't win all the time. Screams behind a locked bedroom door. That evening, her husband disappearing for a cigarette. Everything was up to her and she was only trying to do the right thing.

The lawn chair was no longer on the porch but Father Marc's silver Camry was parked on its asphalt apron and another car was parked at the curb but Harriet could not turn back. Father Marc opened the door in Bermudas and a t-shirt. He was chewing. In the living room beyond, Harriet saw a flashing TV screen, bottles and glasses on a coffee table. A man lay stretched on the couch.

"Father," she panted. "Father, I'm sorry. I had to come back. My son. I hurt him."

"Hang on," the priest swallowed. He disappeared and returned wiping his mouth on a napkin. He came out on the porch and closed the door. "Can we walk a bit?"

"When he was small...things I did. Discipline. Being strict. Maybe too strict. Oh, I don't know." Harriet clutched the priest's arm as he led her down the path.

A woman stared at Harriet out the window of a passing car.

"Don't know what I was thinking! I'd infinitely prefer to see you in the confessional." She made a gesture as if opening and closing the lattice window.

"It's fine, Harriet." He stopped walking. "I'm glad you've come. But I can't solve your problem."

"You can't?" she nearly shrieked.

They were at the place where Harriet had seen the mother and child. The priest steered Harriet back toward her car. "I've met your son or I've seen him, am I right? He brought you to mass when you were convalescing from...."

"Yes, he did. Jim." Why was she horrified that he'd seen Jim?

"We're talking about two different things here, Harriet." The priest opened her car door. "Absolution and forgiveness. I'm your guy for the first but not the second."

Back home, Harriet sat on the porch with Blaster at her feet and tried to still the pain in her heart. She was visited by a scene from the week after her husband died when Jim had stayed on for a few days to help her. One evening while her son was staying with her, she'd begun retelling stories at dinner, of her courtship and early marriage days, then caught herself and tried to steer the conversation back to her son and stories of his childhood but he was silent, his eyes unexpressive. "I don't remember jack," he said, finally, and she changed the subject.

She doubted she'd stop at the rectory tomorrow afternoon when Father Marc said he could spend more time with her, and she was not at all sure she could take his advice and phone Jim. *'Step up to the plate,'* he'd said, sounding awfully much like her son. *'Just a few words could change everything for both of you.'* She detected condescension beneath that advice. Indignation made her pulse quicken and she felt better.

The afternoon had stretched into a long early summer evening. She heard robins, the bright sobs of a cardinal or was it a wood thrush? She no longer knew. Her hearing had been fading for years; soon she would be deaf to the birds. There were benefits to aging, she realized. You expected less of yourself.

5

Pilgramage

Seventy-five was a nice speed for an old woman trying to turn back time. Harriet was headed north on the interstate. Everywhere she looked, nature was ahead of itself. Late April but already as hot as July and with trees leafed out and daffodils long gone. Her husband would have reassured her by remembering another spring like this but Tom was gone two years now. Although she'd stopped the daily crying, Harriet still found afternoons the hardest part of the day. An outing with her dog helped.

She left the interstate and crossed the river at an unfamiliar bridge where the water was ruched satin. Downstream pink spangles were rounding the bend, or was that one of her floaters playing tricks with her vision? At a *Welcome to New Hampshire* sign, she turned onto a secondary road. She was on a yarn pilgrimage, as Tom would have described her search for material to repair her sweaters. Once upon a time such things were available in the notions section of small-town department stores but just try to find them now—like searching for the Holy Grail—another of her husband's expressions. A friend suggested she shop online but Harriet was not about to enter that unknown galaxy. She needed old things now that she was alone and so much was new. She was reading bits of *The Canterbury Tales* with that adorable Rory Matthews who gave a free lecture once a month at the library, embellished with "old spice," as Rory called his research.

"When April with its soft showers," she paraphrased aloud, "has pierced to the root the droughts of March." Were seasons predictable in ancient times? Rory passed over nature in favor of sex and gore.

What a relief to drive north, back into spring! Tulips were bright as Easter eggs outside the Charlestown post office. At Goshen, forsythia bloomed. Soon maple leaves had shrunk to the size of a baby's hand. Blaster propped his muzzle on her shoulder. She passed a scattering of shops: small engine sales and service, tool sharpening, sewing machine repair. Vehicles, houses, people all looked worn down. Here was the New England beyond where most flatlanders had migrated. Agriculture and millwork had collapsed and people made their way as they could in this second and third growth landscape. Harriet found these impressions oddly comforting.

At Paxton, she began looking for Harmony Textiles. "Down on the right by the Industrial Pock," a Quick Stop cashier told her. "You here for the hooking bee?"

Harriet stared at her.

The girl laughed. "Like rugs. My gran is working there this week."

"Oh, you want that other place," the girl said, when Harriet explained her purpose. "Jessicaaaaa!" She yelled to the back of the store. No answer. Harriet watched the girl trudge down an aisle and reappear, panting. "Go back to the center of town, take a left."

Next size comes on wheels. That's what she and her girlfriends used to say about fat people. *No fat woman's dream.* Couldn't say that either, now that it applied to just about everyone. These thoughts distracted her as she passed through downtown and found herself on an unmarked road between scrub woods. Perhaps she should turn around. She was about to pull over when three boys walked into the road and held up the palms of blue hands. She stopped. One boy ran to her window and rapped the glass. His eyes were hidden by his baseball cap and he smiled in a way that alarmed her. The others stood with their hands spread on the car hood.

The boy at her window made a rolling gesture with his hand and she obeyed.

"Scoot over!"

She gave a chirrup of terror as his hand flashed across her lap to unfasten her seat belt and push her into the center and suddenly all three boys were in the car with the doors locked and the windows up and the car moving while Blaster rampaged in the back seat. Hands pushed her forward and jammed her head down and she felt a knife of pain in her back and she cried out. She saw hands tear open her pocket book, her wallet. No one had ever touched these things, not even Tom.

"Help!" she screamed. A hand covered her mouth. She tried to bite a finger.

"Shit!" a voice broke. The hand came away from her mouth.

She wailed, kicked her feet, but she had no strength.

The car was slowing, then idling. Hands passed cards to the driver. Tom's passport photo fluttered near a sneakered foot. They had planned a trip to England. Never went.

"Gimme your pin, lady." The driver poked her side

"Can't," Harriet gasped.

"Hurry the fuck up!" another boy shouted. "Somebody's behind us- FUCK!" The car began to move. "Gimme your pin!"

She smelled body odor, stale cigarettes.

"I'm gettin' hard," said the boy holding her down.

"You stupid fuck!" shouted the driver. He spun the wheel and tires screeched.

These little bastards. This kind of thing happened in poor, violent countries, not here.

"The pin!"

She heard herself say: "I must use the buttons myself. To remember."

"Fucking...fuck." A body writhed over the back seat and she was pushed upright and shoved behind the wheel.

For the first time, Harriet looked at the boy whose lap she'd been forced against. Thin lips, oyster grey cheeks, eyes obscured behind sunglasses. She smelled the odor of poverty and her memory flashed. Maria Tosti, her seatmate in first grade, wore the same dress all year. *Sewed into her clothes.*

"Dear God."

"Do it," the boy yelled.

"Help!" she wailed, but the parking lot was empty and a shade was pulled down on the drive-in window.

Harriet reached out the window and, with a shaking finger, pressed the number pads, heard the familiar beeps while the boy repeated the numbers haltingly. He fumbled in the glove compartment, brought out a pen, paper scrap. A hand lunged through the window to grab the cash. As she was pushed over and forced down again, she saw her pin number written with childish uncertainty. More hollering. Tom's photo was mashed beneath a filthy sneaker. She closed her eyes and repeated the Lord's Prayer as tires screeched.

* * *

How long? Hours? She became aware of silence. Whimpering.

She pushed herself upright and Blaster clambered into the front seat. He licked her cheeks as she wept. Her body hurt but she could move her arms and legs. Her clothes were in a snarl and her pants were damp. She must have peed in terror. She should let Blaster out of the car but instead she stared at a newly plowed field, woods, the lowering sun. A flock of starlings swooped down and began toddling among the furrows, pecking, cackling softly. Blaster sat watching, a thread of drool hanging from his jowl. *Poor old boy.* Harriet turned on the ignition.

The office of the Golden Lantern Motel was empty. Harriet heard unfamiliar music, rhythmic clapping and percussion. On the reception desk, a brass elephant squatted on its hind legs, a pink plastic necklace around its neck. Harriet came closer. The elephant was smiling.

"Good evening, Madam," an Indian man appeared.

"Where am I?" Harriet asked. "Could I have some water for myself and my dog?"

"This is Paxton. Dogs are not allowed in the rooms, Madam."

"He just needs water," she said. The man raised his eyebrows but went for the water. By the time he returned she had decided she would not tell him about the boys, she didn't have the strength. She would just say she'd got lost and it was too late for her to return home and she needed a room.

"I'm sorry Madam. No pets."

Harriet began to weep and it was then that she told him her story.

"This is very serious, Madam. You must go to the police immediately. Or I will call them for you."

Yes, yes, she would do all this but not now. Right now she would call no one, not even her son. Especially not her son. He would only upset her.

"At the very least, call your bank and your card companies."

Yes, all right. She was on hold for a long time and eventually the manager excused himself to finish his chores and she heard the sound of a lawnmower. Her bank was closed but she was able to report her stolen credit card to a sympathetic voice. When she finished her call, the manager appeared. He seemed to have no other customers.

"High season has yet to begin," he explained. "My wife and daughter take advantage of the lull to go home for a visit." It was now past sunset and the manager insisted on bringing her a piece of toast and a cup of tea and Blaster a saucer of milk which the dog sniffed.

"Of course, I will make an exception for your dog," he said.

"You've been so kind," Harriet said. "I wonder if you'd help me with one more thing."

The manager accompanied her to her car where, by its interior light, they found her pocketbook and wallet on the floor of the back seat. Both were empty. Her driver's license was wedged into the passenger seat. It showed a younger Harriet, smiling.

"That's enough," she said. "I can't do more." She meant search for Tom's passport photo.

"How in blazes will I pay you!" Harriet cried, when the manager handed her a room key. Then she remembered a zippered compartment of her pocketbook where she kept an emergency check. She held it up in triumph. The manager put his palms together, turned to the golden elephant, bowed slightly and spoke in his own language. He turned to Harriet and laughed. His hands were still joined in prayer and Harriet found herself doing the same.

"Have you ever visited India?"

"Heavens, no," Harriet laughed.

"Then you don't know how fortunate you are to have real police. Enforcers of the law. In India you must bribe a cop to get any kind of help. Please, I beg you to go to the police tomorrow."

When Blaster had finished lifting his leg, she brought him inside her room, locked the door and set her pocketbook on the bed. She approached the TV, heart pounding. She squinted, pressed Power, heard a sound like stars sifting down in a far universe. She found the remote and clicked through ads, a weather map, stopped at a news program, half expecting to see the three of them being led away, heads down, handcuffed. The anchor was talking about an earthquake. She kept clicking. The new president. She paused. She'd gone against her beloved GOP to vote for him. If Tom had been alive, perhaps she wouldn't have allowed herself to be moved by this man's measured language, his dark eyes. "Do something!" she shouted, then clicked off.

She undressed in the bathroom and carefully folded slacks, sweater, blouse, knee socks, support stockings. For the first time since early morning, she saw her face. Awful. And her body! Her dressing mirror at home was kind. This anonymous mirror showed quivering curtains of flesh. Her belly was the only part of her anatomy that still stuck out. Beneath it, her panties drooped. And the legs. Enough! She turned her back on the mirror, took off her bra and panties and edged slowly under the spray. Thank God for grab bars. She couldn't manage the tiny bar of soap. Hot water was enough and, with it, she could feel her faith in human life returning.

Before the mirror cleared, she dried off, struggled into her panties and bra, found her cane. Even pulling back the bed covers proved nearly too much. Her lumbar was giving her fits. Blaster stuck his nose over the edge of the bed to say goodnight and then Harriet lay still.

Those boys might be very close by. Why hadn't they shoved her out onto the road and taken the car? Why hadn't they killed her? They didn't seem to be armed. They could barely read and write. It all could have been much worse for her. And it would certainly go badly for them if she called the police and they were caught. Tom would say, "Lock them up and throw away the key!" A scene came back to her. The school playground. Maria Tosti throwing stones at her but only after she and the other children began the game—what had they called it?—Knock the Wop.

The room was stuffy. Harriet turned on the light and eased out of bed. With all her strength, she could only lift the sash an inch but a ribbon of cool air reached her and the scent of freshly cut grass. She breathed gratefully.

6

A Castle in the Woods

Rory Matthews had only meant to drop off the book and be home in time for his weekly Skype date with Philippe's mother but Harriet Dawson had waylaid him. Just out of hip rehab, she was getting around on a walker.

"You're like a shot in the arm!" she laughed. "Come sit down!"

Rory handed her *The Decameron*, the next book in his reading program.

"You know Phil and I are going to Monte Carlo next April. Not Italy but close."

"Oh, I love Italy! Never got there. Castiglione will help me imagine. And you, too, of course."

Thank God for Harriet's enthusiasm. She adored him and he her, but today he couldn't stay and get 'all boozed up' with her, as she referred to her late afternoon glass of wine. He told her about Skype and she flapped her hand at him. "Go on your way.

You've thrown me a lifeline." She tapped the book. "But all bets are off if I start going blind."

He knew she was referring to her decision to kill herself when her sight failed. Kindle? Books on tape? No, she liked the feel of pages.

"Before you go, be a dear and bring me a glass of water?"

Harriet's dog followed him into the kitchen where Rory caught a whiff of rot from under the sink, but he wasn't about to take out the compost in his freshly polished loafers.

"Thank you ever so much, I was parched." Harriet reached for the glass of water. "I'll see you next week. Jim will be here, so he can drop me at the library." Harriet held up her arms and Rory bent down and kissed her on both cheeks and they laughed.

The son, Jim. He'd only met him once. Nice eyes. Rory ducked into his Morris Mini, glanced in the mirror, applied lip balm. Winter did that to him but Philippe refused to go south; he wanted to see how much they could save by using their own resources—the lap pool, the sauna. They'd had to let their personal trainers go. Their upcoming trip to visit Phil's mother Betty in Monte Carlo was outside their budget but could lead to greater financial security.

There was something so Doris Day about Betty, so bright and Midwestern and fun and on the verge of tears. She needed him and God knows they could soon need her financial capacity, if Phil would lighten up and be practical. He was the only gay man Rory had ever known who hated his mother. "You're an avaricious hag fag," Phil said just that morning and not for the first time when Rory mentioned his phone date. What a misrepresentation of Rory's empathy and care. If only he could bring Betty and Harriet Dawson together, they'd love each other, but Betty no longer flew. She'd be waiting for him with her glass of white wine and whatever new phone she was using, ready to give him a virtual tour of her latest retail booty.

Betty had moved to this tax haven with her second husband, a French-Canadian businessman who died within a year of their arrival. Phil had adored his real father, a pediatrician who died when Phil was twelve. Betty met the man she would want Phil to call his new father not long after the funeral when she and Phil were on a bereavement holiday in Fort Lauderdale. After her remarriage, they'd moved to Montreal where she'd placed Phil in a boy's school and forced him to add 'ippe' to his first name and to take his stepfather's last name, Beaulieu. As soon as he finished McGill, Phil moved back to the U.S. When Rory met him, years later in Boston, Phil pronounced his name "BaaLEW" but Rory was smitten by his new love's ersatz French glamour, to which he attributed Phil's fine-boned body, black hair and subtle wine sense, even after he knew he was Chicago Irish. Phil made it clear that if their relationship was to endure, Rory must accept his true identify. Rory went into therapy; he struggled with the demoralizing concept of *withdrawing a projection* even as he created a new image of his lover as a man wronged by his beautiful, madcap mother, for whom Rory felt a secret kinship. A decade later, in North Haven, as they planned their civil union, Rory accepted Phil's refusal to invite his mother to the ceremony but later mailed her their wedding photo on the back of which he penciled *we love you.*

Then the stock market crashed. Rory had already been cut back to freelance editing from home and Phil, who was a decade older, had retired from his university job. Phil was stoical about the future. He'd enlarge the vegetable garden, raise chickens and buy a big freezer. Rory said Phil was out of his mind. Even during the height of the easy-money days, nobody could be subsistence gardeners. "If we want to survive, we need to cultivate *Betty*, not food. At least let me extend an olive branch." He was amazed when Phil acquiesced and Rory began his phone calls to Monte Carlo and now, five years into those conversations, they were cashing in their air miles and going to the Riviera for what Rory hoped would be a productive reunion.

Hubert Brinton sank to one knee and began turning over leaf litter, searching for the button that had dropped off as he was closing his fly. Usually, he didn't need to urinate until he reached home, but there'd been no rides and an old Achilles tendon injury was slowing down his walking. A milky late November sun was lowering. It would be dark in two hours. He should be home by now, building up the fire in his stove and heating rainwater for tea.

Usually, he could expect rides quickly in colder weather. Most were men but sometimes a woman stopped, someone close to his own age, and he felt flattered until she began talking and he realized she considered him a charity case, a traveler without a car. Couldn't she tell by his rugged boots, his leather-kneed trousers and backpack that he *chose* to *go on foot*? With his neatly trimmed beard and ponytail, Hubert couldn't imagine how anyone saw him as indigent. In his day, women had even found him handsome. Now, as then, he tried to live as Thoreau wrote, deliberately, pursuing his passion for building, largely in solitude and outside the cash economy.

He pawed the leaves, mistaking stones for the button, then found it and walked back to the road just as a familiar car pulled over.

"My *God*, Hubie!" Rory shouted. "I can't have that stench in my car! And you're still with that backpack! What do you have in there, a decomposing corpse?"

"Iron bolts for the parapet." Hubert ignored his old friend's jibes. "Found them behind the old North Haven forge."

'What's wrong with your paw?" Rory gestured toward Hubert's hand. "That's not *duct tape* you've got on it?"

"Waterproof!" Hubert held up his bandaged hand. "Lucky it happened just as I was finishing the tower. Nearly healed."

"You're still working on your venerable pile?" Rory turned up his own road.

Hubert lifted his pack. "Come out and see. Why not come now?"

Rory had taken Phil to see Hubert's creation once, years ago.

"Is he building it or tearing it down?" Phil asked.

Since then, Rory had given Hubert rides and invited him to their parties but he hadn't been back to see what Hubert considered his masterwork: a many-storied structure created entirely by hand, without the use of power tools.

"Thanks, but not today." Rory stopped beside his mailbox. "I'm late for a phone date with Phil's mother."

"Oh, she of the offshore money in—where is it?"

"Betty is *family*, my dear." Rory pulled a sheaf of catalogues from the mailbox, lost his grip and the catalogues scattered. By the time he finished gathering them, Hubert had disappeared. From Rory's, it was an easy mile through the woods to his house.

Hubert had come to North Haven the year he finished college, having given up his fantasy of translating manuscripts in a rare book room when he discovered that most graduate schools required multiple ancient languages and a working knowledge of library cataloguing systems. He was in Cambridge, selling his homemade Aeolian harps and pan flutes on Massachusetts Avenue, when he bumped into Rory, a friend from high school days, who offered an alternative. Why not move to Vermont where it was still possible to live cheaply in a beautiful place. Rory had just arrived in North Haven, where he was editing a magazine on country living although Hubert couldn't remember him being interested in rural life, or ever lingering out of doors, unless for drinks on someone's porch. Lonely, having just broken up with a girlfriend, Hubert was grateful to follow Rory.

He rented a room on Main Street and found a job substitute teaching at a local boy's school. He was appalled by the bored, manipulative students who called him Hubie Dupe within his earshot. After enduring daily humiliations for one term, he was on the point of fleeing to a monastery in Barre or, if the monks wouldn't have him, checking into the state mental hospital, when he encountered Rory at the Sap Bucket Tavern. During his twenties, his prospects and his state of mind could change in a moment, and so it was that he accepted Rory's inebriated offer to live at Fern Hill, a newborn commune near West North Haven.

Hubert remembered the three years he spent at Fern Hill with increasing fondness the farther they receded. Summers seemed perpetually warm and sunny with the occasional drama of a thunderstorm ending with a rainbow over the woodshed.

Winters brought deep snowstorms followed by blue and gold days and frigid starry nights. Requirements for acceptance at Fern Hill were few: know how to cook something edible; clean up your own mess; be picturesque. He was always available to wash dishes, stack wood, sweep the kitchen, and his lentil and dried apple soup became unexpectedly popular. His shyness made him a good listener, a rare asset around the kitchen table. He chose a room away from the social hubbub of the main house in a former tack room in the barn that he electrified with an extension cord run through an apple tree to the kitchen. He loved the way morning sun fell on his narrow iron bedstead, straight-back chair and table. He found an apple crate for his clothing and acquired a reading lamp by trading a pair of leather pants he'd bought with a birthday check from his parents.

Hubert thought about his parents as little as possible. "I was a mistake," he explained to Rory. "A freak of nature." His mother had been fifty when he was born and his sister already out of college and married. Hubert attributed his shyness to having been raised alone by a series of elderly babysitters.

Hubert's parents arrived at Fern Hill unannounced one August morning during his first year. Hubert was as usual wearing a suede loincloth he had made himself and a sleeveless bathrobe belted with rope. He took his parents to the barn and showed them his room where he had scattered the floor with dried herbs so that their healing aroma was released as he walked on them.

His mother rolled her eyes. "At your age, what could you possibly need to have healed?" His parents were unimpressed by his projects: a grape arbor, a beehive oven and, in the outhouse, a stained glass window. His father paced around the dooryard with his hands clasped behind his back. Finally, he spoke. "We really cannot support this." Hubert was financially disowned.

"The swine!" Rory yelled, when Hubert told him. "They're blind to your talents."

The night after Hubert's parents left, he joined everyone stretched on the grass to watch meteor showers, then returned to his room to inhale the scent of thyme and begin a poem titled "Castle of the Misbegotten," about a man who wanders in search of a home "made from the living woods." That autumn brought a grand harvest. He and Rory made pumpkin pies, and spent late nights drinking homemade beer while Hubert drew plans for his fantastical house in the woods. Winter was bitingly cold but steamy and raucous indoors. When heated rocks in his sleeping bag proved useless against subzero temperatures, Hubert gave in to Rory's urging and moved to the main house, where a girl named Kathleen soon joined him in his bed. After blizzards, everyone rushed naked from the sauna to roll in the snow like nymphs and swains, while above them stretched the ancient pathway of the gods, the Milky Way.

The Fern Hill years now seemed to him like a myth that ended when the property was sold. After Rory met Phil and moved back to Boston, Hubert thought he'd never see him again. He and Kathleen had moved to town where Hubert found occasional carpentry jobs, helped a local mason repair stonewalls and kept working on his house plans. Kathleen lost interest and moved away but Hubert was content to spend evenings alone, reading about the building techniques of the ancient Egyptians and Mayans. He met a young couple willing to let him use a former hunting cabin on the edge of their land while he created his dream. He knew from his reading that ancient people spent their lives within a five-mile radius of their home. North Haven was four miles from his house site and Hubert was prepared to walk.

Over the years, the property changed hands, new owners required rent but continued to allow Hubert to expand his stone and log structure. Eventually, he needed to buy more expensive hand tools, replace a wheelbarrow. He had never been seriously sick in his life but his teeth were beginning to go.

He was nearly destitute when a letter from his sister arrived at his post office box, followed by a thick envelope from a law firm in Connecticut. At the end of his life, Hubert's father had revised his will so as to provide his son with a modest cash inheritance. Then followed months of anxious trips to the post office until the estate was settled and Hubert could close his post box and savings account.

"For that, you need to come inside," said the teller at his bank's drive-in window when Hubert requested $30,000 in twenty-dollar bills. Since a customer had complained about his body odor, Hubert preferred to do his banking outdoors.

Money reeks Hubert thought, as he crammed taped bundles of cash into his knapsack. At the hunting cabin, he concealed the bills in a spackle bucket he used as a foot stool. When he heard on someone' car radio about the increase in North Haven house robberies, he decided to lock up his tools and keep as much of his money as he could carry with him in his knap sack.

The day he moved from the hunting cabin to his castle, a journalist stopped by and asked to take pictures for a photo essay.

"Just don't use my last name." He couldn't explain. "Sort of a tradition with me."

That night, he lay sleepless, trying to remember everything he'd told the journalist. Had he revealed too much? Had the photos given away his location? What was he afraid of? He couldn't say. But when he stopped at the General Store the following Saturday, he felt a rush of pride at a feature headline "A Natural Born Builder."

"That's your place?" A girl was looking over his shoulder at the paper. "My boyfriend and I saw it when we were hiking last week. Awesome! Do you have a Facebook page?"

Hubert laughed.

"You ought to let people see what you're doing. It could be become a big thing."

As he was leaving the store, he was startled by a familiar voice. "Hubie!" Rory Matthews was taping up a poster for his reading program. "My *God*. You're still *here*. And the article! *Fabulous*." Rory was amazed that he hadn't run into Hubert sooner, they lived so close. He'd moved back to North Haven ages ago with Phil. They were looking for someone to build them a chicken coop. Would Hubert have time?

Hubert thought of himself as an artist rather than a finished carpenter. He suggested a fieldstone foundation, shingled slab board sides and a thatched roof; but Rory and Phil had researched predator control and wanted a cinder block footing, insulated walls, glazed windows and a shingle roof. A hen palace.

The job took Hubert the rest of the summer, if he included the number of times he tore out work that wasn't up to their standards. Sometimes Rory would call him in for lunch. On other days, Hubert could hear arguments that sometimes culminated in the slamming of a car door.

"It's all about Betty," Rory confided, one afternoon when Phil had roared off in a rage. Rory brought a lawn chair and a bottle of wine down to the chicken coop. "I just want to put Phil in the picture, literally. All I did was ask him to show himself to his mother on Skype. Is that too much to ask? It's *not* about her money. She's his *mommy*. He's lucky to have one. As you know, mine's been dead for eons."

Money? Hubert was nonplussed but moved by his old friend's tears. The two of them were a bit drunk by the time Phil returned.

A few weeks after the job was finished, Hubert was walking past the house on his way into town as Rory bustled out with his iPhone held high. "And here's the creator of our very own chicken house! Hubert, say hello to Betty!"

"Howdy." Hubert had never been filmed by a phone.

"And now—" Rory was on the move. "Let's go say good morning to the chickens! Hubie, you come too!"

The hens were clustered around a scattering of corn in the sunshine. "Betty, meet Barbra!" Rory pointed the phone at a handsomely speckled hen.

Phil appeared, still in his pajama bottoms, holding a cup of coffee and a check. "Sorry for the delay." He handed Hubert the check.

"And here's the man of our dreams." Rory turned the phone on Phil.

"Hello Mom." Phil yawned, smiled.

"Look how beautiful he is, Betty!" Rory was beginning to weep.

On the way back to the house, Rory clutched Hubert's arm, whispering. "That's such a breakthrough for Phil and his mother. Your being here helped."

Hubert said he didn't do anything.

That December, Rory and Phil invited Hubert to their annual solstice party. Hubert washed up in a tub of lukewarm water and dressed in his newest sweater. He packed and repacked his knapsack, attempting to make the money less conspicuous.

At the party, as he was prospecting around the buffet table, Rory grabbed his elbow and pulled him into the hall. "I'm worried about you!" Rory stood so close that Hubert could smell his friend's cologne. "You're too thin. And why are you dragging that filthy bag in here?" Hubert mumbled about needing an extra sweater.

He recognized Matt Lebow, a town official who had given him a few rides. Matt held a can of Coke in one hand and a thick slice of ham in the other.

"Hubert. You're last name's Brinton, right?"

Hubert said it was.

"I don't think I even knew that." Matt bit into the ham. "A few days ago, something with your name on it come into the town office."

"Me?" Hubert felt a stab of anxiety.

"It's your property." Matt narrowed his eyes, chewing. "You want to stop by and pick it up?"

Hubert said he would. *Property.* Hubert owned no property and he owed no money. He agonized for weeks and, in January, finally went to the town office. Matt wasn't there and an older woman gave Hubert the envelope which he stuffed in his pack. Back at the cabin, he tore open the envelope, saw the words "Internal Revenue," and threw the envelope and its contents in the stove.

For the first time since he'd moved to the woods, Hubert became sick. He lay in bed for weeks with a fever, dragging himself to the stove to throw in more wood or outside to relieve himself or to bring in a bucket of snow to melt. *It's the money*, he thought. The stress of seeing those papers had compromised his immune system. In his delirium, he imagined that the sound of barking dogs was a search party coming to drag him off to jail.

Hubert was sick for the remainder of the winter. He was too weak to break up the ice dams forming on his roof and, during thaws, water ran down the inside wall behind his bed. He was still coughing in March when Rory picked him up one morning as he was going to town for supplies.

"You look *terrible*. And still carrying around the poisonous sack!" He and Phil needed a house sitter who would also care for the greenhouse and chickens while they were visiting Betty. Could Hubert do the job?

"You're a genius and I love you but if you make a mess of our house Phil will divorce me." Rory was not smiling. "The build-up to this trip has been a nightmare."

Hubert was too grateful to be offended by Rory's outburst. He didn't have the energy to fix his roof, let alone clean the dangerously clogged stovepipe.

Hubert had never been away from the castle overnight. He'd built a hiding place for the money beneath his elaborately carved floor and he moved his bed to cover the spot. Then he began to worry about a house fire. There seemed no way that he could feel secure about leaving his money. He would need to bring it, as he always had. Over the years, the rubber bands holding the bundles of $20 bills had dried and snapped and the bills had fallen loose. He did his best to smooth and press them down to make room for his clothes.

When he arrived at their house, Rory and Phil were in the middle of an argument as they loaded the car. Rory turned and surveyed his friend's appearance.

"How do you feel? You still look a bit peeked. And we can't have that thing in the house."

Hubert set down the pack and Rory showed him to a little bedroom in the basement with a nearby utility sink, toilet and shower. Hubert should stay out of the more elaborate bathrooms upstairs.

"No sauna or pool either," Rory added. "I'm sorry, but Phil set the limits. Go over the list I showed you. Do the daily drill. Eat that chicken soup in the fridge, it contains valuable enzymes." He lowered his voice. "And pray for us."

The first shower Hubert had taken in many years filled the basement with steam and used up all the hot water. He came back upstairs in a daze of relaxed warmth. On most of his other visits, the house had been too crowded with people for him to see it properly. He walked from room to room, turning on lamps, looking at the bright artifacts of Rory and Phil's life. Phil's cello case and an antique bronze music stand. Rory's baby grand piano covered with family photographs. A collection of ceramic frogs. In the master bedroom, a wall of photos chronicling their life together. Ceiling to floor bookcases. Paintings everywhere. In the kitchen, ferns raised fronds toward a skylight. He turned on halogen lights over sleek appliances, counters, a long table where he was charmed to see a single place set with a plate, mug and silverware. Off the kitchen was a sitting area with a fireplace and a pair of armchairs. A charred log and ashes showed that the fireplace had recently been used and the wood box was full. Hubert decided that this would be his resting place. With central heating, he needn't use much wood but, on his first night, a fire seemed appropriate.

Having got a blaze going, he sat back in an armchair and looked around. A sparkle in the corner caught his attention. A liquor cabinet held glittering bottles and decanters. Wine glasses hung from a rack beneath shelves of drink tumblers. A snifter caught his attention. He picked it up and held it to the light. A winter woodland scene was etched with great finesse into the glass: hemlocks; pines; a ridgeline and, below it, a fancifully turreted house with smoke rising from a chimney. The most interesting bottle in the cabinet was the crystal decanter with a silver collar inscribed *BRANDY*. Hubert brought the bottle and the snifter near the fire. He poured brandy and settled himself in the armchair.

It was now full dark and, as he looked out the sliding glass door toward the garden, he saw a reflection of himself: a gray-haired man sitting before a fire holding a glass. He preferred beer, but brandy seemed the perfect accompaniment to his first evening. Warmth gathered in his chest as he sipped. He felt a rising sense of euphoria and poured himself another drink. He looked proudly at the darned toes of his socks, his muscular calves, his scarred and calloused hands. He poured more brandy, spilling a bit as he twirled the snifter, admiring the etched scene. In an age of profligate materialism, he had created a handmade castle in the woods. He gazed at the fire through half-closed eyes.

A sound woke him. He'd forgot to close the chicken house! And his pack was still on the front step. He rushed outside, retrieved the pack and set out downhill. A spring wind roared in the trees and a sliver of new moon appeared and disappeared behind clouds. He could barely make out the dark shape of the chicken coop as he made his way unsteadily in the dark. A gust caught him from behind and he tripped, landing on his hands and knees. His pack ripped open as it fell and rolled. Bills scattered like autumn leaves. Hubert stared, unable to grasp the scene. Gradually, he relaxed onto the ground, breathing in the elixir of damp earth. His money was blowing away.

7

Glory

Tina Shaw lies awake listening to the rumble of the town sand truck as it passes, shaking the house. Tina rents a double-wide from her grandmother who raised her after Tina's parents disappeared. Tina owes two months' back rent but right now she's not thinking about that. Nor is she dwelling on the fact that she was just let go at Foodies, the box store in Greenfield. Instead, Tina is planning her eight-year-old son's singing career. The first snow can do that to her: fill her with hope.

But a worry bubbles up: Madison's music teacher, old lady Tucker, the one who got Tina expelled just short of graduation for cheating on the state exam, is still running the school Christmas pageant. Miss Tucker must be a thousand years old by now but Tina hasn't forgotten what happened to her. Life is unfair and borrowing a few answers on the state test was a way of leveling the playing field, only it didn't. To this day Tina does not feel that her mistake fit her punishment: being kicked out and not graduating with her 8th grade class. Flunking summer school because of mono and starting high school late and then everything kind of breaking down after that.

Now her little boy is in the same school and with the same teacher who gave Tina so much grief. What does her son need? Answer: Confidence. Respect. Everything his mom never got. Here's the deal: Tucker owes Madison on Tina's behalf. Madison's shy, like his dad, only worse. He's small for his age and he cries easily. Tina's Gran went to the meeting at school about bullying but it didn't help. Madison needs a glory day before he gets out of North Haven Elementary. So far, the only thing he's good at is music and this is where Tucker comes in. It's her job to make him feel like a star.

Lying on the recliner in her snow-lit living room while her own bedroom is closed off to save heat, Tina imagines her son singing a solo in the winter pageant. Madison has been talking about the show for weeks. His clear little-boy soprano nearly breaks her heart as he sings "Rudolph the Red-Nosed Reindeer" while he's playing in his room.

Tina needs to talk to Tucker. God knows, she's seen her often enough over the years and always avoided her, to the point of getting gas at the other end of town if she notices Tucker filling up at the Shell. Tucker's come through the line at Foodies but never to her register. Maybe she's been avoiding Tina, too. Now that Tina's lost her job, she can't use work as an excuse to stay away from the school. Except that she's *way* late with her plan. The Christmas pageant is the day after tomorrow.

She fires up her old laptop, something Maddy's dad Chad

brought home and, like most of his gifts, it's never worked right. While she waits for hell to freeze over, Tina peers out the window. While she lived here, Gran was a tag sale magnet, which doesn't entirely explain the presence, among the whirly gigs and gazing balls, of gas grills and snow tires and ski mobiles and two generations of kids' swing sets and an ice fishing house on wheels. It's not that Tina loves to live surrounded by all this stuff but she can't imagine the yard without it, just as she can't imagine living in North Haven without all her relatives, many of whom she doesn't particularly like. Hey! How did new PVC pipe get to be over by the hot tub liner? An early Christmas present from Chad? He's wanted to come back since she kicked him out a year ago but, sorry, a thief is not a role model for her son. She knows Chad loves her but he has a bad habit of taking stuff that doesn't belong to him, like the copper in one of Gran's air conditioners. But Tina doesn't have time right now to worry about Chad either. She has to stay focused on the email, if she can work herself up to write it.

To Miss Tucker. You may think you don't know me. ...

Delete

Hey Miss Tucker. Madison Chapman needs your help. ...

Delete

Miss Tucker, My son Madison is singing in your chorus. I know it's late but. ...

By the time Tina presses *send*, the morning's first cars are passing the house.

"Mama." Madison pads into the living room and holds out a paper. "I forgot this."

Tina's heart speeds up again. She should have checked his backpack and here it is: the list of what he needs for the pageant.

"Don't worry, Maddy." She measures out coffee and heats up her son's oatmeal. If everything happens for a reason—which she believes—then she was laid off just before Christmas so she'd have time to shop for Madison's pageant costume. But with what money?

* * *

Lucille Tucker's never-fail sleep trick has stopped working. For years, she's been able to put herself to sleep by imagining herself flying over the dirt roads of North Haven, descending to look at each of the town's one-room schoolhouses. On this December night of what Lucille hopes will be her last year before retirement, she swoops down on Schoolhouse #5 where a couple now raises goats, cruises above #3, recently vacated by a summer renter, hovers above Schoolhouse #1, a yoga studio painted with rainbows. #1 is where Lucille spent K through 8 in the last class to graduate before the Central School opened.

Sometimes she gets no further than #1, drifting off to sleep thinking about her old teacher Miss Vivian Sanderson, a tiny woman with a hatchet profile and a foghorn voice. Eyes in the back of her head the kids said. "Who IS the king of glow-ree?" Miss Sanderson bellowed, reading from the Old Testament each morning. "The Lord of Hosts. HE is the king of glow-ree." Miss Sanderson was Lucille's ideal of a teacher. She loved her old lady lace-up shoes and her tweed suits that probably dated from World War II. She loved her flowery language and her easy command of power. Miss Sanderson maintained order with the threat of a yardstick smashed on fingers. *If only.* Now the kids are snider, more arrogant every year. Even the smart ones are indifferent, eager only to dig out their cell phones. Lucille finds herself cutting corners on assignments, glancing at the clock as much as the kids do, while the younger teachers exhaust her with their professional jargon and their so-called innovations that seem to her like reinventions of the same old wheel.

Dawn. She might as well check the weather. She can see it's already fouling up and she still hasn't put on snow tires. She opens her laptop. New message. She doesn't recognize stardust@yahoo.com. Subject: **my boy has talent!** Spam. Delete? She opens. *I need to see you about my Madison Chapman. 12 noon today is only time I can make it. Tina Shaw.*

Terror shivers Lucille's arms and chest. One student can spoil a class, make a nightmare of a teaching year and, for Lucille, that student was Tina Shaw. Cheating on the state exam was the final straw. Still trying to justify her accusation, Lucille ticks off Tina's offenses: never paid attention in class, when she bothered to come; mostly gossiped or slept; oblivious to discipline; showed no sign of having done the assigned reading.

Then came the state exam. Tina's work was suddenly excellent, with an answer pattern similar to her seatmate, an honor student. Lucille had almost taken the coward's way out, let the cheating slide, pass her out of the class and out of the school but the ghost of Miss Sanderson would not allow. So Lucille took the exam to the principal. Tina stonewalled but Lucille's word held.

Then later, the parking lot scene: from behind her: "You bitch!" and she was being strangled, jammed against the side of her car. "You've got no proof!" Another teacher, Bill Jarvis, showed up and pulled Tina off. By then it was clear that, proof or no proof, Tina would be expelled for assault. Lucille was weak with relief. She'd never again have to deal with this person. Of course, she'd seen her over the years at a distance. Tina had settled into the anonymous hoard of former students that populated minimum wage jobs around town.

Lucille tries to form a mental image of the little Chapman boy. Small. Blond. Not at all like his mother. Weak learner but not failing. He's in the other section so Lucille doesn't have to deal with parents. She's seen the boy with an old babe in stretch pants and a big spangled sweatshirt. Built like an oil burner, probably a grandmother or, the way generations overlap around here, a great-grand. Lucille can't recall a single conversation with the child.

* * *

Tina hopes a hot shower will relax her. All she's had is coffee since breakfast but she's too keyed up to eat. After she puts Maddy on the school bus, she changes into a V-neck sweater that shows off the new snowflake tattoo on her collarbone. She brushes sparkle on her cheekbones and reapplies lip gloss. She coils her hair into a twisty so her silver hoops swing free. She tugs high boots over her jeans, zips up her vinyl parka with the fake fur collar. The boots and parka date from a shopping spree with Chad a few years back that he's probably still paying off. Should she call him? No, she needs to meet Tucker on her own.

* * *

At her classroom desk, Lucille stirs powdered creamer into

her coffee and tries to remember. Was Tina's class ten years ago? There's a new principal now and Bill Jarvis, her rescuer, has moved out of state. Nobody here would remember Tina Shaw's assault, nobody would support her. Lucille slides one hand around her neck. She remembers the affront of Tina's sharp young breasts against her own fallen bosom.

A woman stands in the doorway, closes the door behind her, strides to the desk and stands over Lucille. She's heavier and her eyes are puffy but Lucille recognizes the eyes.

"Hello, Tina." Lucille rises, extends her hand.

Tina steps back. "You disrespected me but you're not going to disrespect my son."

"Nor would I." Lucille reaches to pat Tina's arm.

"Don't touch me!" Tina snaps. Lucille feels her bowels lurch.

"The school hasn't done nothing to help my son. In the show tomorrow, you need to find him a solo to make him feel good about himself."

Lucille stares. A buzzing exhaustion is settling over her panic. "If you'd come sooner… but it's too late to make changes—"

"It wasn't too late for you to get me kicked out!" Tina widens her eyes so that Lucille sees the grains of mascara in the corners. "*It's the least you can do after the way you messed me up.*"

Lucille leans across her desk. Does she have the strength? "I will try to help your son," her voice is hoarse, almost a whisper. "Provided our conversation is concerned with Madison and *only* Madison."

Tina brushes hair from her face. "So, what're you gonna do?"

The anger in Tina's eyes has changed to something closer to desperation.

"All the bad stuff seems to happen at this time of year. I've hated Christmas from when I was a kid. But it shouldn't be that way for Maddy. I just want him to have. ..."

She trails off. Lucille sees the beginning of tears and her heart smites her.

"I'll ask Mrs. Bradley to let Maddy out of class this afternoon. I'll find him a solo and we'll practice together."

"He's so shy." Tina is weeping now. "And I know he's sad. He gets it from me."

"I'll sing along with him, and he'll get the hang of it." Lucille feels warmth flooding her chest. "There's nothing like a performance to make a child feel proud." She finds a Kleenex, hands it to Tina.

"I just don't want him to get so sad that in a few years he turns bad."

Lucille takes this in.

"You are a good mother," she hears herself say. And then to make it stick. "I don't have children. I can only imagine how hard it is."

"Yeah, well." Tina rolls her eyes, laughs.

* * *

Tina on a roll: rushing home to improvise the reindeer suit; rubbing brown magic marker on her son's camouflage pants; pawing through drawers to find his brown Bruins sweatshirt. If she can buy those clip-on antlers she saw at the Dollar store, he'll be all set.

Tina loves the Dollar Store, knows the aisles by heart. Candy and party favors and jewelry near the check out, crafts and paper flowers and costume bits on the far wall, with knick-knacks scattered through each aisle to tempt her if—say—she's picking up a six-pack of kids' socks and she spots a pair of cherubs holding a soap dish that could double as her earring tray. Holidays keep the inventory moving. July 4th isn't past when scarecrow lawn figures show up; then red and silver tree ornaments appear before Halloween. She isn't even sick of Christmas when out come silver Valentine's balloons followed by green beer steins and shamrocks mixed with Easter grass and candy eggs.

"We must've run out of those antlers," says a girl Tina hated in high school.

"Can you check in the back?"

"I know we're out of them." She snaps her bubble gum.

To make things worse, here comes Kim Chapman, married to Chad's brother and no fan of Chad's. Kim walks around all snobby in her Frye boots that are probably handed down from one of the people she cleans for.

"Hey." Kim stops, picks up a pack of twinkle lights and Tina does the same.

"You copying me?" Kim laughs her way into a cigarette cough.

"The one thing I come here for turns out they don't have." Tina hitches up her pocket book.

"What's that?" Kim puts down the lights, shakes out her mop of red hair and pulls it back into an enormous rhinestone banana clip that gives Tina a wicked case of the envies.

"Reindeer antlers. Madison needs them for school." Tina glimpses horse manure and hay stuck to Kim's boot heel.

Kim stares, then a smile dawns on her. "I just saw a pair of those antlers in my girls' room. You can take them. They won't care."

Tina protests. Kim insists. "Gives me one less thing to throw out later."

Classic Kim remark. It's hard to thank someone who's only giving you their crap. "He needs them by tomorrow." Tina adds.

"Hey, no problem!" Kim calls from the checkout line. "I'm going right by your place later. I'll drop them in your mail box."

Tina lines up behind Mrs. Sampson who has a shopping cart full of caramels.

"Turtles are dead easy," Mrs. Sampson says to the old lady ahead of her. "Just melt your caramels in the microwave and pour them over your pecans. Then pour on your melted chocolate. If I didn't make these every Christmas, I'd lose my happy home."

Happy home. *Who says stuff like that?* Gran used to make peppermint flavored Rice Crispy squares every Christmas. Tina throws two bags of caramels in her basket, then thinks about the price of pecans and chocolate, puts back the caramels and takes a box of candy canes.

On the way home, she passes a big guy she doesn't recognize inflating a wobbly six-foot Santa. It's only 2 PM but a giant plastic candle glows on the front step of the Brewster's. Candles shine in every window of Harriet Dawson's old house. Tina loves that look. As she nears her own road, she spots a solitary figure walking. Hoody hides his face but she recognizes the shoulders. She slows to avoid spraying slush, lowers the window.

"Get your PVC out of my yard." The way she's caught Chad off guard, she can't help smiling. She opens the door and he climbs in.

"Mind dropping me at Ace's? He's welding one of my struts." Chad pushes back his hoody and gives her that midnight eye sparkle.

"Then I could stop by?" he adds. "I have something for Maddy."

"And take that PVC while you're at it." She's watching the road so she doesn't get waylaid by his eyes.

"That pipe is so I can fix your hot tub. I know you've always wanted to be, soaking...." Chad's voice gets silly-soft, "Under the stars...in your redneck tropical paradise."

"*Shut up!*"

They laugh.

At home, Gran's old Civic is parked in the dooryard and Tina finds her unloading grocery bags in the kitchen.

"Praise the Lord they had a sale on wings and thighs so I bought double."

"Hey, that is just so nice! Thanks." Tina hugs her. "Chad'll probably try to get himself invited to dinner."

"Well, I am *glad*!" Gran puts her arm around Tina. "Forgiveness is a blessing,"

"Didn't say I was forgivin' anybody," Tina replies. Gran considers any man better than no man. Case in point, Gran's current boyfriend, Ed. She could have set the bar higher. Tina's never heard Gran say a word against Chad which puts her in a class of one.

When Madison jumps down from the school bus, his father, mother and great grandmother are standing by the mail box. Tina holds out the reindeer antlers but Madison runs past her into the house and Tina follows.

He dives under his bed covers. "I can't sing in front of people."

Tina rubs his back, struggles to hold back tears.

"Why does she want *me* to do it?" Madison weeps.

"Because you love to sing and you're good at it." Tina whispers.

By the time Madison calms down and Tina lures him out of his room for a candy cane, Gran has gone home and Chad is in the kitchen lining up chicken wings in a baking dish. Madison runs to his father and begins jumping up and down, tapping him on the back with the candy cane. Tina watches this scene. How can she deny her son his heart's desire, even if she doesn't trust this man?

After dinner, when Tina shows Madison the modified reindeer outfit, he bursts into tears.

"*No way*! I don't want to be an oddball." He throws the sweatshirt on the floor.

Chad's peering in the fridge and Tina feels the old anger. "If you're looking for more beer, there ain't any."

Madison glances at her warily and she sees his father's eyes.

"I'll make a run." Chad picks up his hoody.

"We don't need more beer around here.

Silence. Standoff.

"Okay then buddy!" Chad turns to Madison. "Let's you and me go over to Walmart and find you a real outfit."

In spite of what she expects, an hour later they come home, and in runs Madison with a new pair of brown overalls and a work shirt like his father's. Chad stays in his truck with the motor idling, not trying to sweet talk his way into spending the night because he's house-sitting for Tessa Cates while she's in Florida.

Tina feels her stomach tighten. "How do you know her?"

Chad explains that Tessa's boyfriend arranged the deal in exchange for Chad taking care of the poultry. "They've got a bird zoo out there or whatever you call it where the birds have their own—" he shapes the air—"house."

Tina falls asleep imagining how Gran's ice fishing shack might be fitted out as a chicken coop if Chad moved back in. She spends the next morning driving around on nearly no sleep and no gas looking for job vacancies and finding only one: shelf stocker at the Dollar Store. She applies and they want her to start, like, yesterday. Tina tells the manager she can't begin until the morning. "My son has a big part in a show at school tonight. I can't miss it."

She goes home, changes, takes a Benadryl—poor man's tranquilizer Chad calls it—and arrives in the Central School parking lot as it kicks in. She steps carefully out of her car and onto an inch of fresh snow. Headlights catch snow sparkles. Christmasy! The Benadryl makes her feel as if she's pushing her way through a giant Freezie. She passes people she's known her entire life and doesn't have to greet, she can just give a half smile.

The vestibule windows are decorated with paper snowflakes. A young guy she doesn't recognize opens the door and she's hit with warm cinnamon and cocoa smells from the 8th grade bake sale. She recognizes Kim's daughters over by the food table with their friends. She doesn't know the little guy with the Got Math? button; he must be the new principal. She recognizes Mr. Dolan, the janitor, but no teachers.

"Looking good." Chad appears at her side. And here come his brother and Kim.

"Maddy's got a solo."

"Well, good for him!" Kim says. For a change, her eyes are smiling.

Tina spots Gran, on a cane, coming through the door with Ed, both in their matching Harley jackets.

"Thank the Lord for getting me here in one piece. Fell over his dog." Gran pokes Ed who laughs. "Where's my Madison?"

It's always about you, Gran. "Where do you think?" Tina snarls. "With his class." Gran looks hurt.

"That's new." Tina adds, by way of apology. She touches the plastic Christmas corsage on Gran's jacket and out buzzes a digital version of Silent Night.

"I told her it sounds like a mosquito," Ed says and Gran laughs.

The gym is smaller and brighter than Tina remembers but the decorations are just about the same. The star bursts hanging from the fluorescent lights flash like disco balls. She feels a muffled version of the jitters rise as chatter dies down and the principal comes out on the basketball court to welcome everybody, then goes to sit at an upright piano. Tina can't believe it: a principal who isn't just stuck in his office punishing kids; he plays piano!

The kindergartners straggle to the center, each child holding a cluster of jingle bells. Shepherding them is a big woman in a Santa hat with a long grey ponytail. Jeezum! Tucker is wearing the same outfit as yesterday, the same style that Tina remembers from all those years ago: long denim skirt, bulky sweater, clogs.

She's such a dog but look at how she smiles at the kids like some kind of giant elf.

The kindergarten finishes Jingle Bells and Tucker is herding kids in and out, conducting songs, managing skits, quieting the audience for a 6th grader to read his poem about building a snow fort.

"I'm waiting for a little Christ to show up in this Christmas show," Gran whispers.

Overtaken by memories, Tina has stopped paying attention. Her father at Christmas: scarecrow thin with a graveyard laugh. Dirty fingernails. Her mother: hair stuck together in strips like Gran's ribbon candy. The house cold but filled with flames at night. Matches, lighters, candles. Ice on the inside of the windows.

"You okay?" Chad puts his hand on her back.

Tina sees the deep worry lines in his forehead.

"Madison didn't ask for any of this, you know." She's not sure what she's saying.

"Yeah, well, he'll be proud to see us all here. And you made it happen." He takes Tina's hand, raises it to his lips.

The principal begins pounding out the familiar tune. And there is Madison, his cheeks brilliant, eyes focused on his teacher as she draws him a few steps forward. *Oh please, please, please.* Tina clutches Chad's hand. Behind her, Kim holds up her iPhone. Gran leans against Ed, trying to get a glimpse. Miss Tucker raises her arms and leads the song Tina always thought was stupid until now.

"...then one foggy Christmas eve—" Madison's clear voice quiets the room. Tina looks at Chad. He's better than his brother and she's better than her mom and together they have a wonderful son.

8

Navigator

Nothing's on so can I tell you a story? Yesterday, I'm heading up I-95 in a monsoon. Driving blind through road splash, passing within a foot of 18-wheelers that could obliterate me if I drift out of my lane. How do I avoid it? My car, source of faith.

Then, on 91, around Hartford, the temperature drops and I'm in deep slush. In the old days I'd 've had an excuse to turn back but I just bought myself a Navigator, little divorce present. This car is my environment. I control the air temperature, the air movement. I control what I hear, what I smell. I see out but nobody can see in, which is how life should be. They can badmouth me but I'm deaf to them, and I can say and do what I want because I'm invisible. I roll higher than everything around me and with those tires my rig could climb trees if necessary. This vehicle is the only place I feel completely safe. Take my Navigator away and I'd die like a pig in the street.

But I make some tactical errors that may be the reason I'm now sharing your hospital room. First, I stop at Tapertown, the candle outlet—open 24/7—like candles are an essential service. They have greeters dressed all in white; angels in stiletto heels. *Welcome! How can we help?* What am I gonna say—I'm here to buy a late Christmas present for a cleaning lady I recently slept with who likes lavender? And I need something for my nieces, so an angel suggests *mood flames*. I go with Tranquility and Harmony. Why not get real and call a candle Rage? Or Despair?

There must be something to this candle thing. When I was a kid, we dipped candles. Shuffling around the classroom in line. Dip, shuffle, dip. Making Christmas presents. I loved it, didn't know any better, and is it any better now? My nieces—you can't surprise them. Stuff means nothing the second after it's acquired.

What if I really *needed* those candles I dipped because I'm living in early America. So I raise cows, sheep, whatever, and feed them stuff I grow myself on land I clear with an axe. I eat the animals—they're my food—and I boil down their fat to make wax. I even make wicks, don't ask me how. Then I light a candle so I can see to dip more candles.

Big mistake getting hung up at Tapertown, wasting valuable time as sleet changes to snow. Cars are spinning out and cops are passing me on the right with their party lights on. Then I make my second error: answering a call from my mother. Can I pick up her friend, lives at the old folks' home, going out to his daughter's house for his birthday. Why didn't I say 'no'?

Point of clarification: I'm coming up here to check out a job and visit my mother. Divorce makes relocation sound good. I doubt I'll fit in here but I'm not exactly a celebrity either, like my clients back in the city. My previous boss wanted us to look like them, share their interests. Bond trading, wingsuit gliding: Google it; fake it; make the sale. Not a requirement up here. The top realtor in North Haven hasn't changed his office décor since World War II. If I stay, I'll need to lower my standards about what's correct. Around here, correctness is farting out the back door of your trailer when you have company.

Somewhere in Massachusetts, Edgar, my GPS voice, goes mute. I'm low on gas, no idea how far I am from the exit. No visibility. Nobody ahead of me. No plowed lane. Snow up to the wheel wells. I'm in a version of the Navigator ad: breaking trail, but without the sunset and the cabin on the hill.

They must build these nursing homes close to interstate exits for the ambulances. Departing my vehicle is a shock. I'm used to a neutral climate. Navigator spoils you that way. Long story short: I'm dressed wrong. My boots are supposed to work in three seasons but *at what latitude?*

In the lobby, an old guy gets in my face. "I 'spose you don't know who I be." *Who I be. What century are we in?* My passenger, Russell Cates. He's wearing a hunting cap with the earflaps down, all ready to go, waiting for the rest of the world to catch up with him.

"Quite a rig!" He loves the Navigator, has no problem hoisting himself up and in. No sooner are we on the road than he makes me stop at the Country Store. The owner sees him and starts laughing. "Who let you out?" He hands her a chocolate and she leans across the counter and gives him a birthday kiss. He's stoked. Then he wants to swing by the firehouse where a guy rolls down the window of his pickup, gets a face full of snow. I recognize him: Matt, always on the scene. "You goin' up to Tessa's? You won't make it." Tree across the road. He wants to be the first with the happy news. Russell says we'll go the back way. To be on the safe side, I switch on Edgar. "Shut off that gabber. You got me." He's insulted by my GPS.

It's dusk and we're passing trailers where TV's are on, and little old houses with dim lights in the back where maybe they're eating dinner, and farmhouses with barns where the windows are steamed up. Russell plays tour guide, knows who lives in every house, what they do. We pass the Grange; he tells me what that is. Been a member since he was young, went to dances there. We pass the library. His dead wife was librarian. We pass the church. He's a deacon. The school. He was on the school board back in the day. He's Mr. North Haven and what am I? I sell houses in places I don't know to people I'll never see again.

Then we're behind a plow and he's describing the finer points of snow removal because he's done that, too. It turns off at Sand Hill where, if I'd been smart, I'd have followed and taken him to my mother's place to wait out the storm, and I might not have ended up here, hooked to these machines. Turns out Russell's short cut is a 45-degree unplowed uphill through forest. Everything's cool until we reach the top and I must have tapped the accelerator because we start doing 360s and the weird thing is it feels so peaceful, just a quiet waltz in the snow that ends head first, buried in a ditch.

"What'd you go and do *that* for?" His idea of a joke.

I try my cell. Nothing. We can't sit here running the engine waiting for somebody to find us while we asphyxiate. Russell says we're only about a mile from the house, we can walk. Yeah, right. It's now dark. He says we'll see fine by "snowlight," whatever that is.

Abandoning the Navigator has got to be one of my life's starkest moments. If I have any power, which is questionable, I feel it draining away the farther we go from my vehicle. I take one last look and click the remote lock and see the taillights flicker under the snow and hear that little answering beep and I start losing my shit in a big way. I spared no expense, gave that car everything: front and back air bags; the newest anti-theft system. I just had the doors and hood armored, put bulletproof glass in the windows. Russell pats my shoulder. "Simmer down. Your buggy's not going anywhere." He does not get it.

So it's up to our knees and within minutes, we look like a couple of snowmen in one of those snow globe paperweights and my feet are icing over. At least I remembered my hip flask. I'm taking swigs, Russell's popping chocolate, never stops talking. He's 82 with lungs like a whale.

"So, you're visiting Harriett," he says. And here's where I make my biggest mistake. I begin *sharing*. A word to watch out for. I tell him about the divorce, being fired, selling my house. And now I'm carless. "Boy, is the Devil chasing you!" What am I gonna say to that? We're quiet for a while which is good because I'm out of breath. Then he says, "North Haven's not a bad place to be," but I'm not listening because sweat bullets are running down my face and I think I'm gonna puke. I feel a pain like somebody's tightening a steel belt around my chest. I sink down to my knees, snow up to my waist.

I'm not a moron. I know I'm having a coronary. Russell helps me get under a pine tree where the snow isn't so deep, says we'll "shed up" until I catch my breath, and I'm chanting "hospital hospital hospital." He tries to feel my pulse, loosen my shirt. He gets me lying down with my head on a bunch of branches and my feet raised on a log. My life is ticking away and he's mumbling about how he doesn't know when they'll plow this road. Then he leaves me to go get help and I'm alone.

Now what you need to understand is that I spend most of my time by myself but I'm surrounded by video monitors, cells, TV, traffic, houses, malls. Under the tree is different. I have nothing to compare it to. Alone. The real deal.

So I start listening and what I hear is the snow hissing like zillions of teeny ball bearings. The wind kicks up and the trees roar and I'm inhaling ice crystals. A tree branch lets down an avalanche. I can hear my heart beat which scares the shit out of me. I can hear myself swallow. I start talking, just to hide the sound of my heart, and what do I say? What anyone would say: *Don't let me die.* No idea who I'm talking to.

Something amazing happens: that belt of pain loosens so I relax and begin thinking about wild animals. Bears must be hibernating but what about other stuff, vicious with sharp teeth; what about coyotes? Wildcats? Crazy backwoods rednecks?

By far the scariest thing is what's happening inside me. I'm starting to shake and then gradually the shaking stops which I've heard is a sign you're freezing to death. Then I can feel myself disappearing the way I sometimes felt as a kid alone in my bedroom. I'm shrinking to a speck and becoming part of everything. I'm desperate to bring myself back, so I start talking: *Don't let this be the end of the line. I want to change. I want to be a better man.*

Then I hear the sweetest sound: internal combustion engines.

Light strobes between the trees. I see golden eyes: a snowplow and a skidoo, coming closer. Russell's riding shotgun on the plow, leaning out the window.

"Jim Dawson!" He calls me by my name! I've never heard my name as it sounds at that moment, a name I'm proud to own. Push the Kleenex closer, will you?

I recognize Matt and the state cop who came around after my mom's break-in. They wrap me in a silver thermal blanket—warm as I've never felt warmth—and slide me onto a stretcher with skis. They smile down at me. "Take it easy, Jim. You're okay" They're happy I'm alive! Then I'm sledding behind the ski-doo, lying on my back staring into the snowflakes.

9

Cosmic Dust

Crystal was a smart girl who never put herself forward and by the time she reached high school, she was told she had a social anxiety disorder. Crystal didn't own a cell phone, only used the computer for the online card catalogue and preferred to write in cursive, which got her in trouble with her English teachers who told her she'd never survive in college without a computer.

Crystal was accepted at the one college she applied to, but left after the first semester. Her suitemates were three blond, tanned cheerleaders from Connecticut who lived on Jello shots and diet Coke, talked too fast for her to understand and ran around at night. She saw only one other girl in her dorm who was shy—but maybe not—because halfway through term that girl moved into an apartment with her boyfriend.

Crystal had always had a hunch that she was a throwback, born into the wrong family and the wrong time. She needed a farm family, stable and hardworking and, if religion was thrown in, she didn't object. Her parents, Patty and Leon, descended from such families but that life was long gone. Although Crystal had grown up hearing that her parents' high school love was star-crossed, she'd never known them when they weren't in the process of breaking up or reuniting.

Crystal's mother, Patty, ran an astrology 'practice' as she called it, which brought people into the house or on the phone, and now the internet, at all hours. People came to Patty when their lives were in flux—a word that Patty liked, 'because life is change.' Crystal noticed that her mother talked to these people in fantasies. "You aren't working for the CIA, are you?" she asked a girl who drove up in a fender-less Pinto. "No? Well, I see where there might be work for you in our nation's capital."

Crystal's father, Leon, was a tombstone carver at Valley Monuments, a job that brought in fairly good money which, after he left the first time, Patty hired a lawyer to be sure she got some of. This was while Crystal was in elementary school. Now she was nearly 40, living at home, working at North Haven Greenhouse. Her one attempt at moving out had not gone well. A coworker agreed to rent her a room; but the woman's boyfriend was a bodybuilder who walked around the house in a scarily small piece of underwear, lifted weights at all hours and insisted that Crystal's food not touch his tubs of protein powder in the fridge. When she stopped sleeping, she decided it was simpler to live at home. She continued working at the greenhouse and chauffeuring her mother whenever Patty lost her license for DUI, while what Patty considered her daughter's greatest talent Crystal admired least.

From the time she was small, Crystal could find lost objects. Wallets, credit cards, a fancy earring. Once a diamond drill bit went missing on Leon's work site and Crystal found it nearly hidden under the rear tire of a forklift. In elementary school she found the only cassette recording of the eighth-grade talent show, after it slipped behind the microwave in the teacher's room. When the school secretary lost her engagement ring after she took it off to wash her hands, everyone figured it was stolen but Crystal found it in her wastebasket. Kids asked her to find scarves and gloves so they wouldn't get in trouble at home. When their parents began calling her for help, Crystal discovered that most people's houses were a mess but she was afraid to tell them: "clean up and you'll find it." She couldn't risk them being pissed at her. To find, she needed to feel calm and just drift around, not thinking, not pushing herself, until the object revealed itself. She didn't need to *do* anything.

When Crystal dropped out of college, Patty started pressuring her to turn finding into a career. "Get yourself a spot on North Haven TV. Like Antiques Road Show only you go where people need you." Crystal said she'd rather die than be on TV. Plus, finding wasn't rocket science. There'd been finders in her family for generations but nobody made a living at it. She'd heard of a long-ago aunt who could put her hand on whatever of value people lost back then—a gold piece or a thimble or a locket containing the hair of a dead child.

Now people threw away so much and had so much more stashed in self-storage. Imagine noticing if you lost a button. And look at the yard sales and all the crap Patty liked to stare at on eBay. Worse yet, look at Patty's house, Crystal's house, she hated to admit: the walls covered with spirit quest posters and quotes about maximizing potential and breathing and how everything was already perfect if you paid attention, while at the far end of the living room, a pig slept in a dog crate, snoring softly and running its snout back and forth across the metal grates when it was hungry. Patty's spirit objects covered every window sill and shelf. Along one wall, milk cartons were stacked to the ceiling, stuffed with hard copies of people's charts from back in the day, more recent astrology readings on cassettes and CDs identified with a rainbow of post-its, and that was just what you saw when you opened the front door. The house, like the rest of the world, was smothered with trifles. As far as Crystal was concerned, her gift for finding would soon be obsolete, probably already was.

Patty called Crystal a medium but Crystal preferred the more neutral 'finder'. When someone lost a flash drive, Crystal didn't channel a higher intelligence.

"You can at least advertise," Patty nagged. "Use it or lose it. And jazz yourself up."

Crystal liked to be comfortable: loose jeans, big sweaters and work shirts in winter; long t-shirts in summer.

"You aren't going dyke on me, are you?" her mother wanted to know. "Because that's not in your chart."

Crystal didn't want people seeing her body. She hated her mother's bouncing cleavage under tie-dyed tank tops and spandex leggings. Patty looked like she was dressed for a workout but she never worked out, just stayed hunched over her computer or flopped on the sofa in front of TV smoking her menthols.

Crystal loved her chickens and her garden where she grew

outsized pumpkins and zucchini and sky-high pole beans. Her secret ingredient was tombstone dust, a byproduct of the granite and marble her father worked with. He brought it home from the quarry in freezer bags that, small as they were, just about pulled Crystal's arms out of her shoulder sockets as she carried them from the car to a dry place under the front porch. She'd heard about the dust's properties at the greenhouse and Leon made sure his daughter got first dibs on the pile that formed beneath his grinder. He told his coworkers: "That dust has the density of one of our far-off stars." Nobody expressed interest, so Crystal stretched the dust with dried manure and sold it at the farmer's market as Cosmic Dust.

One Saturday in May, a man with a beard and a wide brimmed straw hat approached her table at the market. He spent a long time reading her poster and fingering the display sample before he reached in the pocket of his work pants, pulled out a leather drawstring bag, counted out a stack of quarters and pushed them across the table to her, then carefully stowed the bag of fertilizer in his knap sack.

"Nifty for my potatoes." He grinned. "I'm much obliged." And then he winked.

Crystal reddened as if she'd been kissed. Her heart pounded as she watched the man walk through the parking lot up to the road. She saw his broad shoulders, his high-topped work boots and the old timey way his suspenders buttoned onto his pant waist. She felt pressure in her chest as she thought of all the things they might have talked about if she'd dared to speak.

That summer Patty and Leon descended into daily fights about money and Crystal stayed longer at the greenhouse or out in her garden. Then the fights subsided, as they did, to be resumed later in another form, sometimes involving throwing things or slapping.

One afternoon, she came home from work and her parents hunkered over a bong in their usual spot on the couch.

"To keep the wheels on this thing we have to reinvent ourselves." Leon pointed to the smoking tube as if it contained a solution.

Crystal reversed direction. "I'm going out to water the lettuce."

"Wait—" Her mother choked on a toke. "You gotta. Hear this." Crystal always hated the pause while she waited for her mother to cough out smoke. "Johnny Depp is looking at land around North Haven."

Crystal doubted that but said nothing.

"I read he won't accept a role 'til he's checked his chart."

Leon raised his head from the bong, blew smoke rings. "Astrologer to the stars." He held out the bong for Patty. "It could happen."

"And that's not all." Patty squinted through smoke. "Here's something for you, baby girl. Danny Till's prize blue tick hound is missing and he's got a reward out."

"I don't do animals." Crystal opened the screen door and recognized a figure out on the road. The man with the straw hat was walking past. Before she could stop herself, Crystal waved and the man waved back, paused, kept going. Behind her, Patty was holding out the phone.

Crystal took the phone outside and peered down the road as she listened to Ginny Mott, head of the North Haven Historical Society. Ginny had misplaced a cherished photograph of her late husband and she'd heard about Crystal from her grandniece Kelly. Crystal couldn't tell if her heart was pounding about the man or Ginny's request that she come to her farmhouse on top of Tamworth Hill.

She came inside and tried to sneak past her parents where they were crashed out on the couch, but Patty roused herself. "I saw on the news where they brought in a medium to help with that missing kid up in Acton. You hear about that? Possible foul play."

Leon took the pillow off his head. "If a medium solves that case, they could end up on Letterman but *oh, no!*" His voice rose. "*That* would be *way* outside your comfort zone."

* * *

Paradise. That was the view from Ginny Mott's front porch as Crystal looked out across a mowing and down into a valley to a brook and beyond to a grove of birches. She heard birdsong and the distant sound of someone hammering nails. She peered through Ginny's screen door at a center hall and a polished banister. She rapped an iron doorknocker in the shape of a fist.

"We're in the parlor!" Ginny's voice quavered. "By the back."

Crystal rounded the house and entered the cleanest kitchen she had ever seen. Nothing was new but everything shone like the day it came home from the store: percolator coffee pot, toaster, copper aspic molds, graduated measuring cups and spoons hanging from hooks over a porcelain sink. So this is what *keeping house* meant. She passed a bedroom where window curtains billowed in on a breeze. She was startled to see a flat screen

TV, inert as a black hole in that bright space. Beyond was a living room where Ginny sat on a couch beside a couple Crystal recognized from around town.

"Oh, gosh!" Ginny stood up, reached out a hand toward Crystal. "Did I say today?" She laughed. "We're planning the historical society barbecue today. Must have got myself discombobulated. I'm so sorry Crystal."

Crystal stood in the doorway in mute terror. Near an antique parlor organ sat the man. Of course, he wasn't wearing the straw hat indoors, so Crystal saw his bare head for the first time. His hair was cut in a sort of bob that he tucked behind his ears.

Ginny introduced Crystal to the group. "And you must know Hubert." She gestured toward the man. "He's the youngest member of our board. We're so lucky to have him."

"A babe in arms," said Hubert and everyone laughed. "I believe I met you at the farmer's market."

Crystal nodded. She thought she might pass out from terror.

Ginny patted a space on the couch beside her. The meeting was nearly finished, would she like to stay? Afterward she could 'do your thing' as Ginny put it. Crystal stared at the fine nap of the wall-to-wall carpet.

"Are you O.K?" Ginny whispered.

Could she have a glass of water? Crystal spent a long time in the kitchen splashing cold water on her face. By the time she came back, people were closing notebooks and pushing themselves to standing. A woman she didn't know came up to her—amazing how friendly most old people were—and asked if she'd be interested in joining the board. They were always in need of younger people. Crystal said she'd have to think about it.

"Nice to see you," said Hubert, as he passed her, and Crystal agreed.

When everyone had left—she noticed that the couple on the couch had given Hubert a ride—Crystal returned to the living room.

"It's about so big." Ginny made a rectangle with her fingers. "And it always sits up there." She pointed to one end of the mantle. "I can't imagine what's become of it. I know where everything is and it's always been... ..... I depend on seeing him." She wiped her eyes.

Crystal asked if she could sit on the front porch for a moment and then walk through the house. Ginny said of course, she'd be out back in the blueberries.

Crystal stared across the valley listening to the sibilance of high summer, knowing she was too distracted to find the photograph. But she went through the motions and later asked if she could come back another day. Ginny was silent for a moment. "Just give me a call." She smiled. "And maybe you'll have decided about our board."

She usually gave her parents six months, a year, max. This time they made it three weeks until the fights began. The day after her father moved out again, Crystal was driving home when a voice passed through her like a chill.

"Your life is shit but it doesn't need to be this way." The voice was her mother's.

Ahead of her, she saw Patty walking toward her. She recognized the slantways shuffle. She pulled over, waited for her to reach the car.

Patty leaned in the passenger window, glaring. "I need you to take me for supplies." Her word for booze.

"I'll take you home or to an AA meeting."

"I've done everything to help you succeed, goddamit!" Her mother began to weep.

"Get in the car, Mom." Crystal tried to open the passenger door but her mother pushed against it.

"Okay, Mom. Do whatever." She began to pull away.

"Yeah, be the selfish bitch." Patty was screaming. "I even called the *Acton Register* and that kid is still missing but you won't get off your ass and use your talent to help our family!" Patty walked backwards as she yelled. "I see bad shit coming in your chart!" She lurched around and kept walking.

Crystal had long since stopped believing in her mother's astrology but she wondered what had brought Hubert to pass by the house a few minutes before she pulled up. She could still see him at a distance as he paused to talk to someone in a pickup truck. She crawled under the porch, dragged out the remaining bags of cosmic dust but they were too heavy for her, must weigh more than a dead body, so she ran to the garden for the wheel barrow, piled in the bags and threw her purse on top.

One more thing. She found a Foodies receipt in her purse and a pen and slid a note under the front door: *Please tell Dad: thanks for the stone dust.*

The sun was lowering and the black top was cooling and he was still stopped, talking by the pickup, but that could change at any moment and she needed to hurry. She lifted the handles of the wheelbarrow but kept the back legs close to the ground, the way her father had taught her, to even out the load, as she began pushing, her knees and back bent. It was not an easy way to walk but she wasn't going far.

10

Spring Snow

"Harriet, what on earth are you *doing* out here like Rapunzel?" Rory Matthews puts his arm around Harriet. "My *God!* You're as cold as a corpse."

He finds her bathrobe, wants to take her to Emergency to be checked for exposure—she was locked out since 6 AM—but Harriet insists she'll be fine after a cup of tea. Downstairs, she allows herself to be settled in an armchair, all the while talking about her adventure with the trapped luna moth.

"I just had to free that beautiful creature but then the balcony door blew shut behind me."

"Thank God I was going to the gym early and you know I always eyeball your back yard to see what's in bloom."

"And I'm ever so grateful you did!" She wonders about offering him breakfast. "But I'm taking you from your day and here I'm lolling about and I haven't even made my bed!"

"Where do you get your *enthusiasm*?" Rory reaches for her hand, leans toward her. "You know enthusiasm is a gift from God. *The god within*, from the Greek."

Harriet squeezes his hand. "What a fascinating man you are!" Rory's reading program is the highlight of her week. "I can't wait to hear you on the Greek myths. But this *Beowulf*." She gestures toward a book on the side table. "So brutal. And that mother!"

They unite in a shout of laughter.

He wipes his eyes. "I did so need that laugh. But, would you believe it, my Springfield bunch is mad for Grendel."

Springfield? Harriet flinches, jealous.

"Could I bother you for a little something before I'm on my way?" Harriet assumes he means orange juice but he points to a decanter of sherry. He pours himself a glass and leans close. "I need to talk to you about Monte Carlo and the monster who's ruining my life."

Harriet remembers him mentioning a trip with his husband Phil. Rory is the only gay person Harriet knows although, as a girl, she wondered about Cousin Victor who never married and was always going to Florida with someone he encouraged her to call Uncle Jerry. They seemed so carefree, unlike the other men in her family.

Rory drains his glass. "The weather was perfect and I was in hell." All afternoon he drinks and tells his story. How it was his idea to reunite Phil and his mother Betty after their long estrangement but the Monte Carlo trip was a nightmare. Phil and Betty fell into each other's arms and Rory felt cast out and, after a few days of torment, he made up an excuse to fly home early.

Harriet knows she should put her hand over his glass but she's in his thrall, as she is at book group, fascinated by his voice, his expressive hands as he describes how 'the scales fell from my eyes' when he realized that Betty's money was a mirage he'd imagined from his Skype calls. His horror when Phil demanded they bring her home to discuss her future. As Harriet hears these details she wonders about her own son. Would he open his house to her? Would she want to accept? Soon it's dinnertime and she thaws out two chicken pies but no, Rory can't touch a thing. He slumps forward, mumbling.

"I'm putting you to bed!" She leads him to the downstairs guest room. When she returns to say goodnight, he's pulled the quilt up to his neck.

"So glad we're friends," he whispers. "Wish *you'd* been my mother."

Harriet smiles down at his dark blond curls.

"Will *you* be my mommy?"

"Mommies are somewhat overrated." She pats his head. He purses his lips and Harriet leans down to kiss him and they both laugh.

That night, she lies sleepless. If Tom were alive, she'd never have spent a day with a gay man, let alone put him up overnight. Naturally, Tom was anti-gay. His story about a cousin back on the farm who corrected his mother about the fabric she was mending: "it's not satin, it's *taffeta*." How many times did he tell it?

She makes her way down to the kitchen for a glass of milk and here is Rory with a blanket around his shoulders.

"You can't sleep either." He joins her at the counter. "They come home tomorrow and the house is a mess. If I don't sleep,

I'll die." He puts his head on her shoulder. "Please help me. If I just had your presence—a benign presence—I know I could drift off."

She cups his face in her hands. "You're just hung over." But she curls up on top of the quilt beside him.

Barking wakes her.

"Hells bells! Jim!" These days, her son arrives in North Haven unexpectedly on real estate business.

Rory drags the pillow off his head.

"Shh!" She creeps to the window as the meter reader's pickup pulls out of the driveway. Shaking, she sinks down on the edge of the bed.

"Harriet! You're weeping!"

She feels Rory's hand on her back and straightens up. She cannot admit to him that she's afraid of her own son.

A few nights later, as she's deep in a new mystery, Rory phones. "I want to apologize for my aberrant behavior but I do believe the alcohol burned some of Betty's poison out of my system."

"You were in no condition to drive." Harriet finds herself pulling back but Rory is inviting her to dinner. He and Phil have made a truce and they want to introduce Betty to a contemporary. Someone interesting. She'd be delighted.

* * *

"Harriet might be a bit outside Betty's experience." Rory arranges vintage mirrored place mats, platinum-rimmed Lenox, appliquéd napkins and his mother's wedding sterling. "You should have seen her on that balcony waving her nightgown with her"—he gestures between his legs—"her dewlap showing." He hasn't mentioned his drunken overnight.

"Betty might surprise you." Phil sets a pot of tulips in the middle of the table.

Rory stands back to admire. He's feeling almost himself after last night's difficulty when he said he wanted Betty 'off the stage.' They'd carried on a whispered battle until Rory broke down and sobbed about being afraid to share his husband and Phil reminded him that Betty was his mother, not his spouse.

Harriet is showered and dressed and sitting by the door with a fleece jacket folded on her arm and her pocketbook in her lap. The lights are set, the dog is fed. She glances at the clock. Waiting: another indignity of old age. When she was young, there was never enough time. Now the smallest outing looms as she gets into a swivet about what to wear, when to begin preparing. So here she is, ready an hour early. Hurry up and wait.

Handsome, handsome. Harriet studies Phil's profile. The strong jaw with a hint of beard, that dirty look that men seem to favor these days. And that straight nose! those eyebrows! He's never seen her house so she's given him the tour. Federal is one of his favorites. The post and beam, a New England temple. What an interesting observation. Harriet can see how Rory is smitten. And those lashes! Black Irish. Do not stare. She turns her attention to the dashboard where a screen in his car lights up with what look like indigo mountain peaks. A neon pink line snakes along the bottom of the screen, begins a jagged climb.

"Kinda cool little option." Phil points to the pink line. "We're at 500 feet and climbing."

"Why, I'd never guess!" Harriet hears her voice more clearly in the closed car. Why is she always exclaiming? Phil, like most young people, speaks too fast and with less emotion. Rory seems to have curbed this trait to appeal to his older followers.

As they chat, Harriet leans back against buttery leather. The car smells faintly herbal. She is looking forward to a drink, dinner, and even Betty now that she's seen her offspring. Rory's view can't be accurate.

* * *

"Nobody can cook in a fur coat, let me take that for you." Rory reaches out.

"Not on your life." Betty clutches the fur. "It's freezing in here."

"We set the thermostat at 75 in your honor." Rory spoons anchovy pasted into egg yolk. He's just decided to name his appetizer Sicilian deviled eggs.

"Scrambled eggs were all Herve cooked." She peers into the bowl. "Awfully yellow. These aren't the cancerous ones, are they?"

Rory ignores her. "Have some of that." He points at Betty's Cosmopolitan. "Maybe you'd be more comfortable in the living room while I finish up here." He takes her elbow and steers her through the hall as Phil's daylights flash into the driveway.

"I don't believe my son is gay." Betty sinks into one end of the sofa, folds her hands into the sleeves of her coat.

"Well, here he is." Rory smirks down at her. "Why don't we ask him."

"Oh, I already have."

* * *

Harriet smiles at her couch companion, Betty, and searches

for a safe conversation topic. "Phil was so kind to pick me up. I hate driving at night."

"Talk about bad drivers, you should see the Riviera."

"I'm fine during the day." Harriet feels herself bristle. "Just don't ask me to—"

"Nobody should. Herve and I had a car service." She opens a silver purse at her feet, takes out a photo. "This is our last cruise on the Belle Betty."

Harriet peers at a photo of a widely smiling Betty in a caftan beside an old gink in sunglasses and yachting cap with his mouth ajar. Mr. Sent-for-and-Couldn't Come. Difficult to tell where the appeal lay. Maybe he was a great lover. Harriet doesn't want the evening to be dominated by dead husbands.

Betty retires the photograph. Now what? Except for color, their outfits are nearly the same. Harriet wears a pale green sweater, and slacks, while Betty's shade of apricot matches her hair. She must have the metabolism of a snake to be wearing that fur.

"What a handsome coat."

"Mongolian fox." Betty snuggles into it.

Ye gods. "Well watch out. The animal rights people around here—"

"I didn't kill it but I did buy it, or Herve did." Betty glances out the window, shrieks. "What's happening?"

Harriet looks in the same direction. "Just a little spring snow."

"This *place*! Aren't you freezing?"

"I'm fine." Harriet bets this babe will be flying back to the Mediterranean before the leaves turn. She notices Betty's silver ankle boots. "Those are cute." She herself wears catalogue slip-ons.

Betty crosses her ankles. "Phil said bring boots and this was what I had. How do you stand it here?"

"How are you ladies?" Phil comes in taking off his apron and sits beside his mother. Harriet watches him turn Betty's gold chain so the clasp rests at the back of her neck. Now he's tucking in the label on her sweater. Betty ducks her head onto his shoulder and Harriet feels a shiver of embarrassment to be witnessing this intimacy. She reaches for her glass. Usually sweet drinks don't agree with her but this one goes down like fruit juice.

One of the dining room walls is decorated with an elaborate plate rail like a tiny balustrade, supporting a collection of fussily decorated mauve china that Harriet wouldn't give houseroom.

"When we met, Rory had a passion for Limoges." Phil gestures at the plates."

"—to be replaced by my passion for you." Rory sets bowls of asparagus soup in front of Harriet and Betty. "Freshly picked and puréed ."

"Herve hated asparagus." Betty sniffs the soup.

Rory rolls his eyes at Harriet, disappears.

"Well, this is lovely." Harriet doesn't think she's ever eaten a man's cooking if she omits all those shoe leather steaks Tom grilled. She hasn't finished looking around. Oriental rugs, polished hard wood, crystal, mirrors, candlelight. Almost too beautiful.

"They say they can't pay their property taxes but you'd never know it." Betty opens her purse, takes out a compact and lipstick.

Harriet is silent. Best not to speculate about other people's money as much as she'd love to.

Betty finishes with the lipstick. "Phil tells me you have a son. Just the one child?"

"Yes." Harriet still feels unsettled about Jim since the other morning's false alarm.

"So, we're the same." Betty's purse makes a loud snap.

Harriet turns so sharply she can feel a nerve twinge down her neck.

"Is he gay?"

"My son? Great heavens, no!" Is this woman losing her marbles?

"Philippe says he's gay but really it's the other one's idea." Betty picks up her empty cocktail glass. "I could use a refill."

"You bet." Trying to change the subject. "Refill."

"It's a thing. They're all doing it. How do you know your son doesn't think he's gay?"

Harriet is beginning to feel annoyed. "Well, he and his wife are divorcing."

"What does that prove?"

Harriet takes a slug of her drink. *In another life I'd toss this in your face, you mouthy dame.* She holds the glass out to Betty, who accepts it, swallows the dregs.

"What's got into those boys? They've been disappearing on me all day."

Betty picks up a spoon and taps her water glass.

In the kitchen, plating is at a standstill as Phil tries to reassure Rory.

"She's mischief," Rory whispers. "I don't know how much

more of her baiting I can take before I get her a room down at the New Englander."

Phil whisks salad dressing. "Nothing will happen. Just clear the soup bowls, please." And then, to Rory's back: "I've done everything I can for both of you, so if anyone has a right to freak out—"

Phil brings in poached salmon and greens as Harriet exclaims and Betty worries about her ability to digest so many vegetables. Against Harriet's protest, Rory pours everyone a glass of wine and refreshes the women's cocktails. "What shall we talk about?" He looks around the table with a smile Harriet recognizes and isn't sure she likes. Silence. "I know! We'll each tell a little-known fact about ourselves. Phil, let's start with you!"

"No." Phil's tone makes his mother look up from her plate. "It's your idea, Rory, you begin."

"Well." Rory clasps his hands. "A little-known fact about me—and I use the word 'fact' loosely... ..." He raises his eyebrows. "... is that I love a man more when I feel the relationship is threatened."

"Is that why you're always provoking a battle?" Phil drains his wine glass and pours himself a Cosmopolitan.

"Oh, I used to feel that way, too!" Betty interjects. "About Phil's real father but it was empty worry. And when he died, my God—"

"You ran right out and got another. So much for love." Phil sips his drink.

"Oh, don't say that!" Betty reaches across the table, knocks over a half full wine glass. "I wanted you, only you, but your father insisted he had to come first, and by the time I was with Herve you were into your girls—"

Phil sighs. "Homophobic revisionism."

"I don't know those words. Do you?" Betty glances at Harriet.

"That's why God made Google." Rory laughs.

Harriet feels she should act as an appeaser but can't think of anything.

"I'm a one-man woman." Betty's voice rises. "And I wish that man had always been you, Philippe, but I needed someone to put food on the table."

"And me to change my identity." Phil takes out a cigarette.

Betty puts her hands over her face. "This is not my son speaking." Looks up. "It's *his* fault." Points at Rory.

"Actually, it's not." Phil lights a cigarette, inhales, blows a column of smoke at the ceiling. Harriet begins to cough and Rory makes a swipe at the cigarette but Phil moves his hand out of reach. "Rory was the first person to know me deeply, as myself."

Harriet glances at Rory.

"Thank you darling, that's very validating, but I don't want this just to be about me." Rory claps his hands. "Let's get back to the question. Betty, it's your turn. What's an interesting fact about you?"

"I'm not playing your stupid game." She begins to weep and Harriet reaches over, touches her shoulder. At all the dinner parties she can remember people stuck to safe topics like disease or town gossip.

Phil comes around the table and, holding his cigarette behind him, bends over his mother. "You know I'll always love you." He kisses her neck.

"Yes! And that's why we need to move on and hear from Betty." Rory assumes a professorial tone. "A memorable fact, please."

"Okay, you asked for it." Betty blows her nose. "I flunked tap dance."

Harriet guffaws but Betty isn't smiling. "Very humiliating for a little Evanston girl to be stuffed in the back row without tap shoes." She glances pleadingly at Phil who has returned to his seat. "Your father was the first person who made me feel pretty. See?" She turns to Rory. "We're not so different. We all want the same thing."

"I'm not sure quite what you're referring to." Rory is not smiling. "But yes, it would be pretty to think so. Someone said that, the 'pretty' part and I can't remember who, it's part of a novel—oh yes—someone in Hemingway."

"Now you're mixing me up!" Betty says.

"Why don't you come with me?" Phil beckons and Betty rises unsteadily.

"Well, in that case, Harriet... ..." Rory lapses into a Scots accent. "Why don't you and I take a wee breather out the back."

Harriet grips his arm and he leads her through the kitchen to a mudroom. "You'll want this." He pulls down a jacket for her and opens the door. Harriet is startled by whiteness. She sees her breath cloud, smells the metallic thrill of snow on new vegetation and then another sharper smell.

"Try a bit of this." Rory offers her a thin cigarette. "No? Well, then just lean closer and take a big whiff." He chuckles, holds the joint under Harriet's nose. Why, she doesn't know, Harriet obeys, coughs.

"This is pretty silly, I'll say. After the kind of evening it's been."

"How has it been?" Rory inhales sharply.

"Discombobulated. Betty isn't the monster you told me to expect. And Phil. First, he's dancing attendance on his mother and they're having a love feast. Then he's making her cry. And I'm not sure I like your game. What's your point?"

Rory laughs. "Just giving us something to do. Something different." He inhales and points at the sky. A full moon has appeared. He lets out a long, shuddering exhale. "La Luna! Everything is beautiful."

"The moth!" Harriet cries. "It can't possibly survive now."

He takes her arm and they pick their way a few feet over the thin layer of snow. "Don't worry. It's probably already laid eggs and died. Moths don't live long. "

Harriet wasn't aware of his nature interests.

"I had a high school crush on butterflies." He holds out the joint but Harriet shakes her head. She's fascinated by the glittering mystery of her surroundings. Newborn maple leaves shed diamonds of melted snow. A garden cart tipped against the side of the chicken coop is significant, she can't say how. And who is Rory: a social impresario or the imp of the perverse?

Back in the dining room, Phil and Betty are sitting side by side in front of chocolate mousse and whipped cream. Betty's expression is calm, Phil's benevolent. Would Harriet mind joining Rory across the table while Betty serves dessert?

"A small helping, please." Harriet takes a seat. "Or I'll be seeing my grandmother."

"I just want to say—" Betty heaps mousse into bowls, piles on whipped cream. "I just want to say that all mothers love their children. Don't you think that's a true fact?" She looks at Harriet.

Dear Lord, back to that. Harriet opens her mouth. "In a word: no." She feels capable of saying anything. "Love can't be predicted before it's felt and it's nearly impossible to describe or understand." Where did those words come from? "I've had a difficult time loving my son. It didn't come naturally."

The table is silent and Harriet sees more is expected of her.

"That luna moth I nearly froze to death saving the other day?" She turns to Rory. "I loved that insect as much as I love anybody."

"Oh, I don't believe that for a minute!" Betty cries.

"Harriet!" Rory throws his arms wide. "You're a pantheist!"

"A moth is just a bug," Betty persists. "Loving a person is much harder."

"No kidding." Phil snorts.

Harriet finds herself swamped with associations, grabs one.

"I'll tell you what I'd been thinking about just before I saw that moth and nearly froze." And she begins the story of a beautiful 8th grader, the beloved eldest daughter of a rich family who lived at the top of Harriet's street when she was a child. The day after this golden girl was crowned May Queen, she came down with a high fever and her parents, Christian Scientists, prayed over her instead of calling the doctor and the girl died.

"They were following their religion even if it led them to let die the person they loved most. Was that love or crime or both?"

"Well," Phil says quietly. "Religion is responsible for a lot of suffering."

"That's why we can't talk about it, not at the table," Betty says. "Not after all this booze."

"We can talk about whatever we want!" Rory shouts. "Let's get back to little-known personal facts. We're only halfway through."

"Really, I don't think I can." Harriet pushes back her chair. "Way past my bed."

But how will she get home? Everyone agrees that no one is fit to drive.

"Isn't your son in the area?" Rory asks. "Oh, sorry, yes, I forgot, the hated Jim." He makes a face.

"Stop! I never said that!" Harriet is on the verge of tears.

Phil takes Rory into the kitchen.

"Cruel and nasty," Betty says.

"It's all right." Harriet blows her nose. "I'm all right." She goes to search for her fleece, finds it in the hall as Rory and Phil return.

"We called you a taxi." Phil cuts his eye at Rory. They join Harriet at the front door and Rory turns on the porch light. Snow has melted from the slate path. As they wait for the taxi, chatting about the weather, Harriet feels her old resilience.

"Spring snow used to be called onion snow."

Really? They didn't know.

"The farmers say it's nature's fertilizer."

"Yes!" Rory waves his hands. "Fertility! New life!"

A minivan slows, stops. Phil and Rory walk Harriet up the path. At the van door, Harriet kisses them goodnight.

"You know we love you," Rory murmurs.

"And I love you," Harriet hugs him.

"Love ya, kid!" Betty shouts from the doorway.

Harriet gropes for the seat belt as the van jounces downhill. She settles herself and stares out the window at dark trees.

"Do any of you?" she asks. The driver glances back at her. She flaps her hand. Just talking to herself.

People say they love each other at the most casual times now. When Harriet was young the word was used in love songs but sparingly in private. Her husband never spoke the word.

11

Alone

Harriet is trying to follow the argument but people keep interrupting each other and her hearing aids can't cope. She knew there'd be trouble when Rory, the leader of their book group, chose something by a Buddhist monk, *The Gift of Generosity*. He and Phil are just back from a Cambodian river journey and he's all fired up about Asia. Her ear is stabbed by a high-pitched metallic squeal. Enough. She picks out the bits of plastic, jiggles the hearing aids in her palm like dice. What bliss to be out of the loop. She'll get a recap from Lucille Tucker on the way home.

"Well that was a waste of time." Lucille peers through the windshield. "And on a nasty night."

"Oh, come on." Harriet's familiar with Lucille's attitude from other rides.

"I'm serious." Lucille ups the speed of the windshield wipers."

You couldn't wander around here with your begging bowl unless you wanted to end up frozen in a ditch. Let's get real."

Harriet guffaws.

"A guy like that monk would be a total charity case and nobody likes a beggar." Lucille pulls into Harriet's driveway, gets out to help her up the path, returns to her car and waits until she sees lights come on. "Keep warm!"

Somewhere near dawn, Harriet wakes. Now she tells herself the daily lie: dimness is just a result of unavailable light, not blindness. To prove it she might as well get up, visit the bathroom, so much easier since she decided to sleep downstairs after knee rehab. She ignores the walker, leaves her cane hooked on the bedstead and moves slowly, one hand on the chair rail.

She squints out the bathroom window. That business behind the trees must be the setting moon but what about the overall sheen? The porch railing, the path, barn roof, mailbox-- everything is covered in a gleaming crust like an undercooked boiled icing. Harriet made just such a culinary failure for her husband's seventieth birthday when there was too much hilarity in the kitchen. Best not to think of those long-ago dinner parties. Present moment is all, or whatever that monk wrote. She's eager to get into Rory's latest book, a trekker's account of nomads in Nepal.

The toilet makes an ominous gulp as she flushes. Pump must be off. She flips a light switch. No power and nothing to be done about it now. She feels her way to the kitchen where she puts another log in the stove. Bravo! Back in bed, she drifts toward a second sleep thinking of other winter storms. City people, even some people right here in the boonies, don't understand that weather, good and bad, is entertainment.

Her son Jim wakes her, calling from Baltimore. Is it true the entire state has been knocked off the grid?

"My phone's working, so how bad could it be?" Harriet sees the flash of Matt Lebow's roof lights. "I'm being plowed out right now."

"You're too old to be stuck up there." Jim wants to bring her south.

"Heavens no!" But don't worry, she'll not do anything crazy like try to refill the bird feeder or drive anywhere; and of course she has enough food, the freezer is bursting.

She's zipping a fleece over her sweater when Matt Lebow enters.

"The whole southern tier of the state is out." He stands dripping in the mudroom.

Harriet thinks she sees a shard of blue sky. "Looks as if the worst is over."

"Just a lull. They're setting up cots down at the church. You might be better off there."

"My bed is here. And my dog." Harriet folds her arms.

"Just a suggestion." He accepts a donut, bites off half. "This might not be the best time to get into it but I thought you'd want to know since you and Tom was part of it before." Finishes the donut. "With what Danny and them said last time, I don't know if it's actually going to reach review ...."

"Come again?" Was it just Harriet or did everyone find this man impossible to understand?

Matt chews, swallows. "I always said Willoughby's 'd be a can a worms."

Harriet remembers. When Willoughby wanted the town to buy his wood lots to begin a land trust, Matt said the town shouldn't be in the business of owning land. Her husband and many others agreed. She thought they were wrong but she kept her mouth shut.

"It's on the agenda next select board meeting." Matt is out the door. "I'll stop back tomorrow with your rock salt."

If Harriet had her way, all land would be conserved, including the 300 acres that her husband considered their nest egg. But Tom is gone.

After dressing and putting a pot of steel cut oats on to simmer, she moves around the kitchen checking oil lamps, candle sticks. Then she settles near the wood stove with oatmeal and Rory's Nepal book. She adjusts the magnifying glass and joins the trekker's journey as he arrives at a yurt and is offered a bowl of yak butter tea.

That afternoon, she moves to her husband's old lounger and puts her feet up. Her dog Blaster comes to nuzzle her hand. She listens to the snapping of the fire and the gentle ticking of the grandfather clock. Why not tell time by the sun, moon and stars, like a nomad. She pushes herself up to stand, opens the clock's cabinet and stops the pendulum.

Ringing. She grapples with the phone. "Right here!" The house is dusky. How long has she slept?

"You nod off?"

Her heart lurches. Why is Jim always plaguing her?

"Still no power?"

All is well, people have visited. Why, thank fortune! Someone is coming in the back door right now. Thank you, darling but she must hang up.

"Thought you might like a ham steak, the last of this batch."

"Is that you, Sally?" She can't make out her features.

"Who else? We've got the generator going if you want a shower."

"Haven't done anything to get dirty." Harriet knows that Sally follows town business so she might as well test the waters. "I'm thinking of going to that select board meeting about the land trust."

"That! It'll never pass." Clattering. "Let me reach this frying pan for you, start that ham."

Okay, change the subject. Harriet laughs. "The more you do the less I can do for myself."

That evening, she dines on ham and fried potatoes, a princely dinner compared to the barley gruel a nomad family eats squatting around the wisp of a yak dung fire. After dinner, she holds the magnifier close to a panorama of a snowy vastness and a solitary yurt. The wind rises, rattling storm windows. Later, in bed, she feels the house shake and thinks of deer pressed close together below hemlock; chickadees clustered deep within tree cavities; mice burrowed in leaf litter and herself, another sheltering animal, generating body heat under her comforter.

Next morning Harriet takes the walker and moves from window to window. She's not so blind that she can't see nature in ruins: trees with limbs snapped or trunks sheared off and, everywhere, branch rubble. What a brutal pruning! The few intact birches are bent double, frozen in gruesome cascades.

A sponge bath and the dishes washed with grey water takes her all morning. At noon, she puts on work gloves, muck boots and ice creepers. She finds Tom's pickaxe and drags it to the door. With one hand on the railing, she chips ice crust to get at the snow underneath. Slowly, slowly she bends down, steadying herself on the door frame, as she pushes snow and ice into a roasting pan. The exertion sets her heart pounding but she finishes the job and pushes the pan over the door jam and inside.

She is lying down when Steve Davis stops on his state police ski-doo.

"Oh, you dear man."

"We've closed the Center Road. Wires down like spaghetti. A miracle your phone's still working. Let me give you a ride down to the shelter."

"I'm better off right here. Look!" She gestures at the pan of snow melt.

"You brought that in yourself? You've got no business out on that ice." He glares at her and disappears, returns with spackle buckets of ice and snow. "This should do until we can bring you a five-gallon bottle." Harriet protests but he shakes his finger at her. "I don't want to be sending first responders up here."

No sooner has he left than Jim calls to rattle her nerves.

"They're saying your county is 'the wedge of darkness.' You need to get out of there."

"You're watching too much television, dear." Differences with her son still sadden her. What would she do if she moved into a retirement place near him? She hates bridge. TV drives her bughouse. Why can't he understand that she and Tom moved north for the challenge. Of course, she's more vulnerable now, that's part of nature, and Jim is just one more challenge, like the ice storm. The monk would agree.

That night, she doubles up on aspirin and reviews her accomplishments. Her heart survived the day but, for a fact, she is worn out. With flashlight in one hand and cane in the other, she makes her way toward the bedroom. Near the wood stove, her foot comes down on a soft—what? She shines the light on a dead mouse lying on its side with its tail curled, eyes closed, as if it were napping in the stove's warmth. Blaster sniffs it and returns to his bed. She nudges the little corpse out of the way. She'll take care of it tomorrow. No. Now. She scoops up the mouse with the ash shovel, opens the stove door and tosses it in, then continues to bed.

Entirely too much is made of death. Sitting on the side of her bed, she pulls her sweater over her head, feels the rush of cold air and struggles with her pajama top. How many billion people live on earth? She slides down her trousers and dangles a pajama leg in the vicinity of her right foot until it catches on her toe, then pulls on the pajama bottoms. Most are born and die in obscurity; a few are chosen by mammon to be envied and mourned yet they, too, will be absorbed back into nature. She keeps her socks on and slides into bed.

That ice chopping made for a good sleep and at 8 AM Harriet is famished. She's bending over a skillet admiring a frying egg when Lucille Tucker calls from North Haven Cares. Are Harriet's meds holding out?

"Oh, yes, thanks. But I never returned that walker you lent me after my new knee."

Lucille's reply is lost as the line goes dead.

"Well, that's that," Harriet looks at Blaster. "Our last link to civilization."

The next days pass quietly as Harriet moves from kitchen to bathroom to woodshed. She tends the stove, thaws soup, washes socks and underclothes in snowmelt and hangs them to dry on chair backs. With a flashlight, she begins hunting in the old file cabinet where Tom stashed a copy of the property deed and the surveyor's map. When Steve Davis stops with more water than she'd use in a month, Harriet is busy with her magnifying glass. Papers are spread over the kitchen table.

"Keeping yourself busy, I see."

"Oh, just reviewing my vast estate," she jokes.

One morning, Harriet peers in the bathroom mirror and barely recognizes herself with greasy hair and soot streaks on her face like a nomad. Rory stops by and is appalled.

"What a mess you are!" He dabs at her face with a damp dishcloth. Ringing. "Your phone is loud enough to wake the dead!"

"That's the idea." Harriet picks up the phone. "I'm busy right now you'll have to call back." She hangs up.

"I'm glad I wasn't on the other end of *that!*"

Rory has dropped by to give her some travel washcloths. And why not let him and Phil make her comfortable at their house. By the time he leaves, Harriet is exhausted from holding her ground. She pushes back in the lounger. Without her friends, she'd never be able to continue living here. She must repay their kindness and her only wealth is land. After she's gone, the developers will be breathing down Jim's neck. People need places to live, but she must make sure her woods and mowings stay as they are for everyone to enjoy. Of course, her son will oppose her.

A noise. As if summoned by her own thoughts, Jim stands before her.

"I don't appreciate being hung up on after driving all the way up."

"Hells bells!" Harriet struggles with the lounger footrest, heart pattering. "I thought the roads were closed."

"I got through. What's all this?" He turns on the flashlight and bends over the kitchen table, picking up papers.

"Don't touch them!"

He glares at her. "What are you trying to do, sell something?"

"The opposite of that and it's none of your business."

Jim squats in front of her, gets close to her face. "If somebody's trying to swindle you, I want to know about it. I have power of attorney."

"You do indeed but only in the event of my incompetence or death, neither of which has occurred!" Harriet's face is blazing. "It's too late in the day to get into this. We can talk in the morning. Your room is made up for you."

He glances around as if to check for intruders. "I'm staying down at the motel."

At the door, he turns. "Dad specifically said not to break up the land."

When he's gone, Harriet tries to still her shaking hands. What would the monk say? *Detach.* She cannot change her son. She must do what she knows is right.

Pounding rouses her. It's too late for visitors but the noise persists. After many minutes, Harriet reaches the door and greets a pair of adolescents. Amanda and Julian have come on a ski-doo from the TV station.

"We'd like to send a crew tomorrow to interview you about your—" the boy looks over her head toward the kitchen—"you know, about your ordeal."

"What ordeal?" Harriet laughs. Of course he means the storm, not Jim. "Well come ahead." That night, she considers what to tell these kids. Cleanliness is less important than kindness. Giving enriches more than owning.

When the room flashes into brightness, Harriet is shocked at how letdown she feels. In the glare of the bedside lamp she stares at her blackened fingernails. With time she'll adjust to her old advantages, but right now she must turn out lights she didn't know were on and get herself cleaned up before Jim arrives.

She plugs the bathroom sink and turns on the tap, but the soap escapes and as she bends to retrieve it the room swings sideways and now she's on the floor with one leg twisted. Nothing hurts but she needs to let her heart calm.

Look how much better she can see with those vanity lights blazing. Bless its heart, here's a spider by her left arm. Amazing the way it moves along all on its own, mysterious and beautiful like everything in nature. And now her hair is wet because—the damned sink is overflowing. Harriet turns on her side. She'll deal with her leg after she saves the spider from the approaching flood. She snags a piece of toilet paper and nudges the creature across the floor to the wall where it begins climbing. Spider Man! Who wouldn't want that power? Now if she can push onto her elbows, she might be able to free her leg.

The phone. At this early hour it can only be her son. After ten rings, silence. Harriet has untangled her leg but can't seem to get up on her knees. Jim will be here any minute, probably thinks she's dead. He might be disappointed. After he leaves, she must call down to the town office about that donation.

The Hystericals

Selected Short Fiction

12

The Cellar

Patrick was awakened by a gunshot. He rolled over, opened his eyes. The roof of the tractor shed began to spin. *PUT THIS SIDE TOWARD LIVING SPACE.* Black lettering on pink fiberglass. The words spun into a cotton candy vortex. He was going to barf.

He shut his eyes, reached over the edge of the mattress, groping. Shoe, ash tray, cigarette pack, books, cans. Salt welled under his tongue. He knocked over empties until he felt the blessed weight of a nearly full bottle. He hoisted himself on an elbow and gulped stale beer, fell back with an arm over his eyes, sparks throbbing behind his eyelids.

The door flew open, smashed against the wall.

"Get up. David's killed the pig."

Patrick eyed Jane, arms crossed and legs apart, silhouetted

against sun. He swallowed bile, gagged, rolled away from the light and spat on a stack of old *NEW YORK TIMES*.

"You're dis-gusting." She glared. Light shone through her dress. He could see the tuft of hair between her legs. She wore ancient Greb Kodiaks. Her heavy blond hair was tied back with a piece of baling twine. He loved her to wrap her hair around his cock. The thought brought on his morning erection, followed by a coughing spell.

"Come on, then." She turned. "If you wouldn't get so *focking* drunk, we could have butchered her by now."

Even cuss words gained status in her mouth. *The English woman.* His friends in Bayonne couldn't believe that he was raising pigs on a farm with someone who sounded like the Queen.

She slammed the door. He lay listening to her boot steps, imagining her long strides, her elegant, filthy legs, as if she were hiking on some moor. One of Chaucer's characters. She'd read him a bit in the original. Sounded like music. He loved hearing her read anything—the school lunch menu from the *North Haven Register*. *Tuna Melt. Fruit Salad. Sloppy Joes.*

A rock hit the side of the shed.

"Up!" Jane shouted.

Relentless bitch. He bent his legs. Knee cartilage creaked. Too much basketball on concrete courts when he was a kid. He shoved off the mattress and raised himself. His vision filled with a snowstorm of dots. He stumbled over stacks of library books and newspapers, gashing his leg on the edge of the wood stove as he bent to put on his overalls. He steadied himself against the door jam and slid into a pair of barn boots, staggered outside into a clump of Jerusalem artichokes and pissed.

"No, no, no, watch the mud please!" Alan's command.

Patrick glanced around as the earth raced in the opposite direction.

"Tent pegs, please!" On the other side of the driveway, Alan was directing something, as usual. The wedding tent. Best to avoid Alan. There had been nastiness last night. What? Alan accusing him of not making his monthly contribution to the farm account. Alan, with his secret vacation stash. He could go sit on it.

Patrick needed something so he could see. Maybe the keg had arrived. He ducked in and out of the workshop, the woodshed. Objects vibrated in the sun, stabbing his eyes. He rounded the house and entered the dank funk of the cellar. The dirt floor was slimy. He grabbed a post, felt for the light switch. Blown bulb, as usual. They'd be better off with lanterns the way Jane wanted. Medieval Jane. A chuckle caught in his throat and turned into a fit of hacking. He spat. Even without the light he knew that in the corner sat the cider keg, now nearly empty. He pawed his way up the stairs, hands on the risers. At the top, he stopped to let his heart calm down. There were Tessa's awful canning jars. Tomatoes like abortions. Beans, watermelon rind with mossy sediment.

He stepped into the hall, past the sound of typing behind Cal's door. In the kitchen, Tessa, in green satin running shorts, bent over the oven, removing bread pans. She glanced at him.

"Well, good morning."

How did she pack so much venom into a greeting?

"Hell-low." He tried to sound jaunty as he opened the refrigerator, felt around. Nothing. He squatted by the counter. His calf smarted. A line of blood had soaked through his overalls. His eyes were level with the back of her knees. Oyster flesh.

"What can I get for you?" Tessa looked down at him, unsmiling.

"Nothin'." He stared at the floor. A speck moved. An ant was dragging a clot of granola many times its size. Dream the impossible dream. The words tracked through his hangover, making him laugh. He bent forward, coughing, palms on the floor, crushing the ant. When he was able to breathe, he asked about the keg.

"After twelve."

The lady is pissed off. He tried to stand, decided against it, pretended to look for cereal.

"What're you doing baking bread on your wedding day?" He hated himself for fearing her.

"Oh, I could do this in my sleep." She turned back to the stove and he saw the frayed elastic of her underpants in the leg hole of her shorts. Where was that bottle? He spied a promising shape behind a leaky sack of beans: an unopened pint of cooking sherry. Answering his prayer, Tessa moved from counter to table. He slid the bottle into a side pocket and pulled himself to his feet.

"Want a slice of fresh bread?"

"Na. Thanks."

In the outhouse, he tore off the plastic cap and poured sherry down his throat, leaned against the window frame while the sherry took the edge off his pain. One more pint might do it. When he opened his eyes, he saw Jane and David in the orchard tying Big Red to a branch of the apple tree. Thunder rumbled.

"Cock sucking son of a bitch!" David spat the worlds as he pulled on a block and tackle. "Fucking son of a whore!"

"I don't know why you think cursing will help." Jane turned, spotted Patrick in the outhouse. "It's about bloody time!"

He tossed the empty bottle down the hole. To avoid running into Alan, he headed for the barn. Suddenly, a miracle. The beer keg stood inside the door. Love returned to the world. Bracing the keg between his legs, he pumped up the siphon and twisted the spigot. A stream of foam shot out. What to catch it in? He looked around. The sherry hadn't been enough to clear his vision. He scanned empty kerosene cans, bushel baskets, a roasting pan full of old motor oil, boxes of dusty canning jars. He grabbed a quart jar, blew into it, raising dust. A spider scrambled over the lip of the jar and he blew it away. He let the foam overflow until clear gold began to rise. He filled and drained the jar twice in long gulps, filled the jar again and turned off the spigot. Beer spurted around the edge of the seal. He bent over the keg, struggling.

"Breakfast?" Alan stood in the barn door. He wore a Mexican sombrero and white Bermuda shorts. "You know we *did* procure that for the wedding guests."

Procure your skinny ass. Patrick picked his way to the back of the barn, around a maroon plush sofa, a collapsed wicker baby carriage, lawn mower, car parts. A barn full of shit and none of it his. Hot light met him at the side door but now he could bear it. As he rounded the pig yard, a piglet trotted to greet him. Others followed.

"Hello darlin'." He bent to scratch under her chin and she shied away, then allowed him to stroke her back where tiny black hairs were beginning to sprout. "We gonna eat your mama." The other pigs butted their snouts against the slab wood fence, oinking softly. *I did this*, he thought. *Raised these suckers so we could eat in the winter and* nobody *helped me.* He was up alone at 3 AM in a northeaster when Big Red went into labor. The piglets were born on the run. Jane bought him a gallon of Paul Masson to celebrate and he came four times the next night, or had that been a dream?

"Let's get on with it" Jane shouted from the orchard.

The body is a burden, he thought, slogging through the pig yard. He was down to one thirty and still his legs felt like cement. He made his way toward the tree where the sow was hanging by her feet.

"Jesus, this is a Christly heavy mother!" David pulled on the rope. The pig's head lolled to one side against a pile of green windfalls. A dark hole above one ear leaked blood.

"Where the knives at?" Patrick stood panting. As a boy, he'd helped his grandfather in Secaucus dress a pig every fall. They worked all night in the back yard while his uncle cut up roasts and chops on the kitchen table and his grandmother wrapped the cuts and ground scraps for sausage.

"In the pail by your foot." Jane pointed.

His grandfather kept the slaughtering knives in a black leather box with a brass clasp. No one else was allowed to handle them. He said that getting your meat was a serious business. After he finished, he boiled the knives and sharpened them and oiled them and set the box on a high shelf where it stayed until next year.

"Give me a hand here." David strained on the rope, trying to lift the sow clear of the grass. His t-shirt was soaked with sweat.

Patrick gripped the sow's haunches and hoisted her until her head swung free. His heart sloshed in his ears.

"That's it." David turned away from the pig, took out a handkerchief and blew his nose. "She's all yours. I'm gonna take a shower, have a drink, and enjoy my remaining hours of bachelorhood."

Patrick glanced at him. *Better you than me, pal.*

"Squeamish, don't you know." Jane watched David walk to the house. She put a milk pail under the sow's head. Thunder rumbled.

Patrick picked up the double-edged knife, felt the blade with his thumb. His heart shook through to his back. His hands weren't so much shaking as flapping.

"That's won-diful." Jane smirked. "A regular Sweeney Todd."

"Listen." Patrick felt his throat tighten. "I'm what you got here in the way of a pig cutter."

Holding the sow by her ear, he drove the knife into her neck where he hoped her jugular was. The cut took all his strength. Her front hoof jerked, catching him on the shin and he jumped backwards. Blood ran down the sow's chin. He jostled and tugged the knife downward until he'd made a longer gash, then pulled out the knife.

"I could use some beer." He didn't look at Jane but she began to move. You spoke and sometimes your words had that effect. Mostly they didn't.

Pig blood pattered, filling the pail. "We eat everything but the squeal," his grandmother used to say. Head cheese, blood pudding, his family loved it all. Blood pudding was a hangover cure. Turned your shit black. He rubbed his hands on his overalls and relit a half-smoked cigarette. He sucked a column of smoke down the center of his body, exhaled heat, steadying himself against the pig and the pig against him, letting the blood empty.

Last fall's slaughtering had been easier. The weather was cool and he'd had a fifth of Wild Turkey. If Tessa and David hadn't decided to get married now, there would be no need for this labor and the danger of trichinosis. He dropped the cigarette butt in the bloodied grass where it hissed, smoldered. He caught a whiff of menstruation, a stench from his boyhood. He'd found an old sanitary napkin in his mother's bureau drawer. The thing was hitched to an elastic belt. Why had she kept it?

"Here's your bee-ah." Jane pronounced the word as if it were absurd. She carried three sloshing jars in a spackle bucket.

Patrick drank down a jar, belched. His hands began to relax. He inserted the butcher knife just short of the sow's vagina and drew the knife downward along her belly until he could fit in two fingers. He shivered at the hot slippery feel of her insides. There was a smell of fresh sex. He slid his fingers along the abdominal sac, following with the knife, careful not to puncture the gut. Blood and water ran down his arm and drained off his elbow as he gentled the knife back and forth.

"Push." He glanced at Jane.

She pressed both hands against the sow's belly as Patrick leaned into her ribs, the two of them struggling to keep the incision closed.

"You cut her bladder," Jane said. "I can smell it."

When he reached the navel, Patrick withdrew the knife. He was seeing spots again.

"'Get Cal," he gasped. "And the hose."

"The hose was never meant to reach this far." Jane stood back. "We'll need to bring the carcass down."

"Just do it, please." Patrick closed his eyes. No one knew how tough this job was. He longed for a quart of bourbon and a mattress. His mouth tasted rank and salty, like pig blood. His left knee gave way and he stumbled, caught himself. The carcass emitted a hiss of bad air and the intestines dangled. Grey hose. The brick colored liver slid out, then the stomach, gall bladder. They made an iridescent pile in the grass. Patrick vomited into a clump of Queen Ann's Lace. When he turned around, Cal was scooping the organs into a bucket of water.

"Thanks, buddy." He'd been wanting to puke all morning. Now he felt stronger. He found another Mason jar with yellow jackets circling, drank. Something bit his elbow and burned. He rubbed the sting.

Cal sawed through the diaphragm, separating the rib cage and drawing down the lungs. He loosened the heart from its sac and plunged it into the bucket.

"For my cats." He smiled up at Patrick. "Now let's hose her down."

Jane was dragging the barn hose into the orchard. Her face was flushed and her dress was smeared with blood. Patrick was reminded of illustrations he'd seen of women in ancient Greece who dressed in animal skins and worshipped the wine god.

"It won't reach," she hollered. "I *told* you."

Cal hacked through the pig's neck. The head dropped and bounced on its snout and Patrick heaved it into the wheelbarrow. He held the sow's haunches while Cal sawed through her rib cage and the silky layers of belly fat to the white spools of the spinal column.

"Now comes the part I hate." Jane made a face. "Thank God you're doing it, Pat."

He glanced over his shoulder at her and she smiled and narrowed her eyes. He held the loins while Cal cut a circle around the hooves. He made an incision from the crotch to the hock. Patrick hacked the skin free from the inner fat while Cal slowly pulled back the hide. Patrick was breathing hard. His arm ached.

When they had worked their way down to the sow's forelegs, they let the skin fall free. They untied the carcass and toppled it into the wheelbarrow.

Patrick walked a few paces away to another tree, turned his back and pissed.

"I'll wheel this stuff down to the fire," Cal said. "If you can take care of the guts."

If I can? Patrick felt a rush of anger. *I can and I do.*

Jane lifted the bucket.

"I'll do that." Patrick reached for the bucket. "You bury the blood."

"Bury! It's the best thing for the compost pile. The worms love it."

Jane's crazy ideas. He sat back on the grass. Cold sweat ran down his sides and he shivered slightly. A joint would help. Simon was down by the fire. He'd have something.

"Yo, Si!"

Simon flipped the hair out of his eyes and looked up. Patrick would still have to walk down there and get the joint. He didn't want to move. He felt in the pockets of his overalls. Nothing.

Something was in the bib. A roach. Cinder of happiness. He lit the joint, swallowed the rest of the beer and gazed out over the farm. From the slight rise of the orchard, the land sloped down to the pig yard where piglets lay in their wallow beside a tangle of blackberries. In the back yard, Alan was sitting on a stump, legs crossed, staring at the tent. As if sensing Patrick's stare, he glanced behind him, rose and walked briskly toward the house. Down by the fire pit, Cal and Simon were laying strips of meat on the barbecue grate. On the far side of the driveway, Jane stood on the compost pile stabbing with a pitchfork. At the center of the scene was the farmhouse, its asphalt siding glittering in the sun. Tessa sat at an upstairs window with a towel on her head, talking on the phone. David was visible through the open window of the outhouse.

Patrick inhaled. The scent of marijuana and wood smoke bound the scene. With the tent, it could be old England. *This is my home.* The thought brought tears into his throat. He could have been in jail if it weren't for this place. Or sleeping under the Pulaski Skyway. Or dead.

In the outhouse, David was sighting down the barrel of a twenty-two.

Patrick stood up. "Hey! Don't start that again!" David was on a kick. Must have something to do with getting married. He had to play the asshole one last time, not that this would be the last time. Men never stopped doing anything. For instance, himself. The number of times he'd promised women he'd quit drinking. Or maybe David really thought he was being helpful, shooting rats in the pig yard. The rats ate the pigs' food. They came in the house and died in the walls and stank, but this wasn't the time to play exterminator.

"Gotcha!" David cackled.

I'm drunk but I'm not a fool. Patrick picked up the bucket of guts and went to the house. In the kitchen, he passed Alan making himself a sandwich at the counter.

"Innards." Alan cringed. "Ugh."

You've eaten worse and liked it. Anger made him assertive. "Give me a hand with the wood."

"Oh I'd love another chore!" Alan patted egg salad onto a slice of Tessa's bread. "The caterers are coming at four and I'm in charge of the tables and by the way—" He raised an eyebrow. "The keg is out of bounds until the reception." He widened his eyes.

My ass. As if you aren't going to get hammered in the near future.

Jane strode into the kitchen, unscrewed a jar and dumped walnuts on the counter.

"Dear, dear!" Alan brushed bread crumbs into the compost bucket and began wiping the counter.

"We've nothing so simple as a nut crackah." Jane went outside.

"Clean up your mess!" Alan shouted.

"I'm not through!"

The Jane and Alan show. Patrick found a garbage bag and dumped the contents of the bucket.

Jane stalked back into the kitchen and began cracking nuts on the counter with the blunt edge of an axe. Each smash set off sparks behind Patrick's eyes.

"What in God's name do you think this is, *The Flintstones*?" Alan rolled his eyes at Patrick.

Not for the first time Patrick amazed himself by feeling affection for Alan moments after he'd loathed him.

Jane swept shells into the compost bucket and began eating nut meats, holding each morsel between thumb and forefinger as she nibbled. Patrick watched her jaw bone flash. He wanted to take off her clothes.

"Drive me into town?"

"And buy you a bottle?" Jane snapped. "I'm splitting more wood for the barbecue since you didn't. You'll just have to wait until the party. Four hours won't kill you."

Patrick picked up the bag of guts and headed for the cellar. He caught sight of himself in a mirror above the kitchen sink: desperate eyes; cheekbones streaked with dirt and blood; black hair to his shoulders and a Rasputin beard.

Down he went, shivering in the clammy darkness. The red light of the freezer flickered, on its last legs. He opened the lid and withstood the gush of cold air, tossed in the bag of organs.

By the cider keg, what did he smell? Probably rat. After pig blood, nothing bothered him. He lowered himself painfully to the floor and felt for the wooden tap. Someone, probably himself, forgot to remove the plastic siphon hose. An image came to him of a rat drowned inside the keg. Never mind. Propping himself against the side of the barrel, he sucked on the hose. In the dim light from a window, outlines became visible. He'd never noticed the massive foundation stones. How had they been moved? On stone boats, with horses. Jane said the foundation dated to before the Civil War. In the old days, everyone needed to drink just to live through the work. Nobody worked now the way they did a hundred years ago

Patrick had worked today. He sucked, letting his eyes wander, relax. There were wooden crates full of glass beakers and condensers left over from David's attempts to make vodka. In a corner sat a cast iron cauldron. Before his time, Tessa had hoped to support them with a candle making operation. Brightly colored plastic toys spilled from a disintegrating cardboard box. Tessa's daughter? Someday he'd have a daughter. He could see her, dark and beautiful; but when he thought of her mother all he could see was his own mother with the scapular medal and the picture of the bleeding heart. Couldn't wear it in the operating room. He put it around her neck before she regained consciousness. "God will bless you. You kept me from harm," she said. Dead a month later.

Farther back in the corners, objects lost their distinctness and became chaotic, sinister. He thought he saw a coil of chain. He took another pull of cider. His head felt better than it had all day. Cal told him that the original house on this foundation had been a stop on the Underground Railroad. He felt in his pockets for his last cigarette. No matches. He'd need to go up to the kitchen for more and already he could hear people arriving to cook. A flash lit up the cellar. Rumbles. More footsteps. Women's voices. The bridal party.

"—looked evrawhere for him!" The wrath of Jane.

"Maybe he's passed out somewhere." Tessa.

"He'd make an excellent lightning conductor." Alan's laugh.

The pounding of new arrivals. Voices blurred. Patrick took another slug of cider. The Underground Railroad. He'd check it out at the North Haven Historical Society.

"I don't see how he can stay here." Alan's voice. "He hasn't contributed one cent to this reception."

"I'd say the pig is a rother nice gift." Rother. Jane was defending him. The future mother of his child.

"Cal did most of it." Alan again.

"Let's not start in." Tessa. "This is supposed to be a celebration."

Of what? If it weren't dirt cheap to live here nobody would.

"Well, all I can say is that we have some very pressing issues to discuss at the next house meeting." Alan's footsteps. Even from beneath the floor, Patrick could identify the snap snap of those little rubber thongs.

"The hardest thing to do in life is to love," his mother said every time he came home with a new girlfriend.

The cider was helping him remember, helping him get ideas. No one was going to kick him out. He'd live in the cellar if he had to. He yawned, sucked on the hose. He'd go back to school, write a book. He had a great subject.

13

Wild Mushrooms

A week before David died, the drought broke and heavy rains were followed by a vast mushroom bloom. Giant white puff balls swelled in the field above the house and a golden swath of chanterelles edged the woods. Tessa described the scene as she looked out their bedroom window. Mushrooming had been one of their shared passions. She cranked up the bed but David's vision was too bleary and the light hurt his eyes.

Tessa hadn't left David's side since he came home from the hospital two weeks ago after rehab—the term was laughable—from another open heart surgery that had been, in his cardiologist's words, "a last ditch attempt." Tessa cringed at the military reference but David was a Civil War buff and the expression amused him. At night, she lay beside him, held his hand and made sure he didn't try to pull the oxygen tube from his nose. During the day she sat by his bed with her laptop. Anne, the hospice nurse, urged her to take breaks and go downstairs where people were cooking, fielding phone calls and visitors, but Tessa refused. She was the thread connecting David to life. She must talk to him, offer food although he hadn't eaten in days, and record everything: his words, pills, sponge baths, mouth swabs. Nothing was beneath her notice.

"Mushrooms. Please." His eyes were closed.

She looked at the nurse.

Anne nodded.

Tessa placed her hand over David's hand, squeezed gently. "Darling, darling." She kissed his temple and he opened his eyes.

"Pick. Lots," he whispered.

In the kitchen, her friends turned toward her as one person. She felt a wave of annoyance and then remembered that they hadn't seen her down here in nearly a week.

"I'm just getting a bit of air." She tried to adjust to the room but the ceiling seemed higher and the light was different. She glanced around, looking for garden baskets. "David wants me to pick mushrooms."

"Wonderful!" Amy, another neighbor, was taking a casserole out of the oven. "Do you want me to go with you?"

"I'd like to be by myself."

The phone rang. Gwen, the home health worker, answered. "Nathan is on his way." David's younger brother was a carpenter near the Canadian border. "And I forgot to tell you, the cardiologist is coming at 4:00."

Jerry was an old pal of David's from their baseball days. Tessa knew that David would perk for Jerry if for anyone.

"Mom, Amy should go with you." Her daughter Madeline had

come down from Montreal when she heard her father's prognosis.

"I'm fine." Tessa found a basket under the dinner table.

"It's hot out there." Madeline gave her David's Red Sox cap.

David's friend Jasper opened the screen door, put down a six pack and folded Tessa in a wobbly hug. "Oh Lord, you're wearing his hat!" He began to weep. "I know he can't handle booze but this is just pale ale."

"Go on, Ma, I'll take care of it." Madeline walked Jasper outside.

Tessa moved through the dooryard, past the day lily border, the woodshed and the first pile of next year's firewood waiting to be stacked, the Japanese knotweed and the rusting rototiller, an artifact from the commune days, the old tractor with a rusted tin can capping the exhaust pipe. Who would cut the fields, let alone fix the mower? She knew what they were saying back at the house: *she'll have to sell this place but it's all she has now. So cruel after what she's been through with his affairs and her raising Maddy alone and the fire and then her car accident. Did guilt bring him back, when he saw her in the hospital? I'll never forget that scene* (this would be Tessa's neighbor Carla). *Then he runs off again for how many years? He comes back and she's ecstatic all over again and now this.* Then a harsher voice: Amy. *When they're old and their health is shot, they come crawling home.* Tessa's friends wouldn't say these things even if they thought them. They'd supported her through everything, as she had them.

Tessa was so distracted that she nearly bumped into the postman's Jeep at the mailbox. Fred, a reformed alcoholic, hung an elbow out the window.

"How are things, if it's okay to ask."

"David's resting."

"Good, good. That's what he needs." He handed her a stack of envelopes and a roll of catalogues bound with an elastic band. "If there's anything I can do, just call." The jeep began to roll while he craned his neck. "I'm praying that he doesn't die on you."

Tessa stared at the retreating Jeep. *Idiot.* Blinking tears, she stuffed the mail back in the box and slammed it shut.

Dying on me. As if David's heart attacks were aimed at her. Everyone still wanted to think the worst of him. She didn't understand forgiveness either but she knew that her longing for her husband, even now when he could barely manage a drinking straw, was stronger than the hurt which, like the pain of childbirth, she forgot each time he came back to her.

When she first met him, he'd stopped her in her tracks. Those straight eyebrows and grey eyes that changed to hazel or green according to the light. Those voluptuously full lips. His kisses. The timbre of his voice. She wrote her song "Old Virginia Furniture" to describe that voice. Connecticut was more accurate but the South evoked beauty and loss. The song still aired on folk stations.

"Divorce was great for your career," Amy once commented. The first time he left, Tessa sat down at the commune's upright and composed "Your Car is the Wind." A musician friend showed it to his band and soon she was writing the band songs about love and heartbreak and reconciliation.

She wasn't like Amy, who ran around on her husband until he finally did her the favor of leaving. Or Carla, who alternately fawned and yawned over Joel, an old gink with pots of money who paid for everything. Or Mindy, a former communard who believed that men had a three-year shelf life. Even Maddy had condemned her father the last time he left, saying she was "so mad I could cut off his weeny."

As she walked, Tessa found herself singing:
Up all night listening
for your tires in the driveway
but that sound of treetops swishing
only fills me with dismay.
'Cause the wind sounds like a car
and I wonder where you are,
king of the fugitive hustle.

There at her feet was a puffball as big as a baby's head. She bent down and placed her hands on the mushroom, gently twisted and broke it loose. The base puckered like the end of a balloon. She put the mushroom in her basket and walked on.

Number one was named Ginger, emphasis on the first syllable, a research fellow at the state library where David worked. Tessa was panting as she walked uphill, out of shape after so many days in the house. She ignored a smaller puffball and concentrated on reaching the chanterelles. Sweat trickled between her breasts. Not long after David moved out, Ginger phoned to apologize. "I know just how you feel; I've been there." Tessa had hung up. Later Ginger came to one of Tessa's singing gigs billed as "Heartbreak Heaven" where Tessa sang "Slow Dance."

Tough Guy grabs you 'til his knuckles turn white.
He drains the bottle, what the heck
leaves purple grapes around your neck.

If she couldn't have him, she could at least write songs that portrayed him as an unlovable thug.

Over a rise, where pasture turned to scrub, Tessa saw the first scattering of chanterelles. She knew that you should leave a third unpicked to ensure future blooms but she took them all.

After she and David divorced, he mysteriously dropped Ginger and married Dolly. Tessa found the name absurd. She pictured an inflatable woman. When David and his new bride bought an ostrich farm, Tessa wrote "Head in the Sand." Meanwhile Maddy was having trouble in school and Tessa spent a lot of time sitting with David in the principal's office and at family counseling. He never challenged her opinions. He didn't want any trouble; he wanted to flee.

At the edge of the hemlock woods lay a congregation of boletes. Like the other mushrooms she'd found that afternoon, they were pristine, unpredated by worms. This bounty must be a sign. Perhaps David would rally. She picked promiscuously, without concern for which variety of bolete might be dangerous to eat. She wandered deeper into the hemlock gloom until she saw what had always eluded her: King Bolete, the great Cepe himself, with a cap like a well-browned brioche over a fat stalk. It took both hands to gently loosen this giant from his seat.

Her basket was full. She set it down and saw, further along, the ancient stone cellar hole. When she and David were young, this was their bower of bliss where they came on hot afternoons. The stones were over two centuries old but solidly set, the good bones of New England. Weariness caused Tessa to lie down and close her eyes. She would just be still for a moment and regain the energy to hurry home to David.

Years after he divorced Dolly and renewed his vows with Tessa, he took up with Alex, their tax accountant, a hefty dame with a bleach job she couldn't keep up with. Tessa had liked her until she discovered the affair and then she called her The Axe. She drifted into a reverie of song:

When I took you back
You confessed to all the facts
Sex in late night library stacks
How ostrich plumes give kinky whacks
But after all our midnight yaks
Once again you broke our pact
Made tracks
In the tax lady's Volvo.
That new car smell is what I lack
So if you try to patch our match
And say you've given her the axe
I'll latch the door and bake a batch
Of dough that lays you low.

She woke with her heart pounding. Her cheek was imprinted with pine needles. She found the basket and returned to the edge of the forest. Down below, the farmhouse windows blazed gold in the lowering sun. As she hurried downhill, she stepped on a cluster of black trumpet mushrooms but ignored them, her foraging passion spent, as more lyrics rose unbidden:

If the wind were your car
then nothing else would matter.
I could cancel that order
for your head on a platter.

She was saddened to think of those lines but at the time they'd sustained her.

"Mom!" Her daughter was running toward her.

* * *

David's was a green burial at the top of the hill not far from where Tessa had picked chanterelles. After they'd shoveled in the grave, Tessa sat in the shade surrounded by friends. A pickup jostled uphill and David's friend Jasper unloaded tubs of chilled wine and a stack of folding chairs for people who didn't want to stand or were too old to get down on the grass. A few people went back to the house to prepare lunch while a stream of late arrivals continued up the hill. Tessa watched all this as through a veil.

Her old commune pal Rory arrived out of breath with his partner Phil. "We rushed back from the Cape as fast as we could but you know the traffic." He knelt beside her. "You've never looked so beautiful. Where did you find those jet beads?" He ran his finger along the fringe of her skirt. "Isn't that true that she's never looked so beautiful?"

Phil nodded.

"How can this be happening?" Rory began to weep. "It's just so totally impossible."

"Life often is," Phil said quietly. They put their arms around her.

Tessa heard the squawk of an amplifier. Down at the house, her old band was setting up. She got to her feet. "Rory," she touched his arm. "Run right down there and tell them no amps and none of my songs." She and Phil descended the hill slowly.

Tessa watched her friends carrying platters of food to picnic tables, creating a party like so many others. Soon she was hugging new arrivals, many of them regulars at her concerts who kissed her and wept. Here was the woman who cut her hair, the butcher from the general store. Maddy stood in the midst of old high school friends. Someone brought Tessa the house phone so she could talk to her brother in California whose plane was delayed, but she lost reception. She accepted a glass of seltzer, a bagel and cream cheese and set them down untouched.

At the far edge of the crowd stood three women Tessa recognized without knowing them. Had the trio become friends or was this an impromptu grouping? In the country, most people knew or knew of each other. Should she move to greet them? No. They would come to her. She watched as they made their way through the crowd. The fat one in the flowing cotton pants and tunic must be Ginger. Alex she recognized by her frizzy hair, now white. That left Dolly, the frail one using a cane.

Tessa straightened her back, sucked in her stomach and made her hands into a little basket that hung at the level of her pubic bone. She narrowed her eyes and formed a tiny smile to show wise, amused equanimity. A slightly brittle Buddha. There was nothing to avoid, nothing to fear.

Ginger was the first to speak. "Oh, Tessa, what a terrible—" She was interrupted by the others. "So sudden...so sorry for your loss."

Dolly moved a step closer. "I was happy for you and David when you finally got back together."

Finally?

"How many years did you rob me of? Let us do the math."

Tessa had planned to remain silent but the phrase composed itself. Dolly began to weep.

"Could I offer you ladies a beverage?" Jasper appeared with plastic cups and a bottle.

"I was just indulging in some harmless graveyard humor." Tessa patted Dolly's shoulder. "Excuse me. My daughter needs me."

"They have a fucking nerve." Maddy gripped her mother's hand. "Do you want me to make them leave?" She glared in the direction of the three women.

Tessa put her arm around her daughter. "The Irish have a saying: 'weddings make enemies and funerals make friends.'"

"That's right." Jasper filled Maddy's cup. "They're just paying their respects."

Amy approached holding a steaming skillet. "Allow me to present wild mushroom ragout."

Tessa admired. Boletes were always a little slimy, but over rice nobody will notice.

David's cardiologist peered at the mushrooms. "I don't recommend serving that to a crowd."

"I love you, Tess, but I'm inclined to agree with Jerry." Carla sniffed the pan. "They do smell wild. "

"I picked them for David," said Tessa. "Put them on the table and they'll get eaten."

That night, Tessa did not want to be alone, so Amy slept on the couch, David's brother put a sleeping bag on the porch swing, and Madeline elected to sleep in the bed where her father had died. Tessa lay awake in the upstairs guest room. Before David's heart condition became apparent, she saw the two of them as a version of their happily married friends, moving into later life with humility and gratitude. His three paramours—if there were only those, which she doubted – were harmless.

Her stomach growled and began to cramp. She'd barely eaten and then only a small helping of the mushrooms. They might be indigestible, nothing worse. How odd that she'd taken that wild cornucopia as a sign of renewal. Fungi fed on decay. She remembered joking with David about the 'corpse finder,' mushroom, named for its tendency to fruit near dead mammals.

She watched out the window as Venus revealed herself, followed by the moon against the background music of insects. David's grave was a dark patch at the top of the pasture. He'd fled again and there he was.

Swept off your feet by Lady Death

The first line of a song came to her.

14

Fire Wall

Tessa was lying on the couch with a magazine open over her face when Amy came to retrieve her pot.

"What does it look like I'm doing?" Tessa muttered, when Amy asked.

The center of her wrath she saved for David's nurse, Ann, who arrived unannounced and gathered Tessa into a prolonged hug.

"I know," Ann whispered. "He left and you're angry."

Tessa pulled away.

"Love never dies," Ann said.

Tessa stalked to the kitchen counter and began gathering crumbs into a pile. "He's a hell of a lot easier to love now that he *is* dead." She brushed the pile onto the floor.

Her great wayward lover was nearby and underground. She'd never again wonder where he was. Meanwhile, she was walking around with her toenails sticking out of his holey socks. She wiggled her stubby toes. They looked nothing like David's slim ones. He used to cut her toenails with his pen knife. Now she'd let them grow into feral claws.

* * *

The next morning, Tessa's college friend Marcia, arrived for a bereavement visit with her new man Dennis. She and Dennis had in common the death of their spouses. No, they couldn't stay over, they were on their way to a rental on the Cape. "We're seeing each other in a gentle way," Marcia said. Tessa took this to mean that they hadn't yet slept together. Marcia added: "When we sit down to eat, two spirits join us on the floor."

"Floor?"

"That's where we eat."

"Ah." Tessa said. "A Japanese séance." But she was curious to meet her friend's new friend, a computer technician.

Dennis was tall and thin with rimless glasses and draw string pants. *Draw string guys,* Tessa stared at the pants. *Guys without flies.* But there was something compelling about how Dennis held her hand between both of his and then stroked her forearm with his long fingers, eliciting a scene that shocked her: those fingers running up and down her body like water.

Dennis and Marcia brought with them a loaf of bread to go with Tessa's soup of indeterminate vintage. She'd discovered it in a corner of her old chest freezer where she'd gone rooting through anonymous chunks in plastic wrap or foil until she found a yogurt tub marked b. soup. Beet? Beef? She couldn't identify the contents.

"Lentil?" Dennis asked, sniffing his bowl.

"Burdock." The name surfaced out of the sludge of memory. "Roasted and pureed."

"Wow." Dennis took his bowl and folded himself cross legged on the rug.

"Please let me offer you a chair!" Tessa urged. "I don't vacuum."

"All good." Dennis said.

As much as Tessa loathed that expression—all good—she was charmed by his dimples. He looked boyish as he smiled up at her.

Marcia joined Tessa at the table as, below them, Dennis took his soup bowl with both hands, lowered his head and lapped the contents.

"It's about posture and the timing of each swallow," she explained later. "That's how he cured his colitis."

Tessa wasn't so lonely that she would tolerate a man who ate like a pet dog. Besides this habit, Dennis seemed agreeable as he chatted about babysitting his new grandson and the walking tour of the Hebrides that he and Marcia were planning. When they were finished lunch, he rose from the floor in one smooth gesture and cleared the table. Not so bad, Tessa thought: a fit guy who loves changing diapers and helping in the kitchen.

After the pair left, Tessa slumped on the couch in a torpor of sadness. It was early days but she knew she would never be able to rustle up a man, no matter how odd, and make the best of him. She stared out the front window where the view appeared as a blur. Not cataracts, too? She squinted, then got up and approached a decade of cobwebs on the screen. Thank God! She should get rid of that screen anyway. She never opened the window. She sat down and slid lower onto her tail bone as words rose:

Vaguely through a window
what do I see?
Nothing as distinct as
The trash you left inside me.
Memories like dead sperm—

She wrote the words on the back of a condolence card from her dentist. Purging bitterness cleared her head.

You chose him even when you knew he was chronically unfaithful, David's friend and lawyer warned her. *Dave and I both have bad track records."*

As if summoned by these grim thoughts, Jasper appeared in an Oxford cloth shirt and tie and clean blue jeans and carrying a briefcase.

"Are you in disguise?" Tessa asked. "Who are you trying to be?"

"I should have come sooner but Tyler surfaced and I needed to get him into rehab."

"Tyler," Tessa mused. Jasper's son by a long-ago marriage. A beautiful lost boy.

"His mom won't have anything to do with him."

"So you stepped up." *About time.* Jasper and David had, in their youth, subscribed to a twisted form of Rousseau's romanticism. Children were born wise and should be left to raise themselves and impart infant wisdom to their parents. After the birth of her own child, Tessa became hyper-vigilant about the infant's welfare. Meanwhile, Tyler's parents were unfazed when he wandered into woods and was found hours or, in one case, days later.

"The experience really opened up his mind," Jasper told David at the time.

"Fatherhood was not your forte," Tessa said, smiling.

Jasper's mouth disappeared into his mustache. "Go easy on me, Tess. You're not the only one hurting." His voice wobbled. "David was my best friend."

"I used to think that, too."

Jasper squeezed onto the couch and moved Tessa's feet on to his lap. "Oh, baby, he loved you so much."

"Don't start." Tessa muttered. "He never hurt you like he hurt me."

The next hour was spent retelling stories and sympathizing with each other's sorrow until Jasper remembered that probate court closed early on Friday and if they wanted to file the will, they'd better move.

"Where'd you get this?" Tessa climbed into Jasper's VW camper.

"Emergency housing." Jasper said, as the van fishtailed onto the dirt road.

Tessa braced herself against the dashboard as Jasper veered down the hill, slowing to eyeball the selling price on a red Camaro parked in front of a trailer.

First stop, the bank to close David's accounts and empty his safe deposit box. Tessa had never bothered to know what David called "banking." In her thinking, money was like cancer, a nasty fact of life that people discussed too much as they got older. Worrying about cancer was a great way of getting cancer's attention.

Tessa was phobic about financial details but she tried to keep one thousand dollars in her savings account for emergencies, an ample amount twenty years ago when David paid the mortgage and the major bills. Every time he moved out, the money stopped and Tessa saved whatever she made singing, ate less, traveled only when essential. She told herself that she wasn't living badly, just differently, that a simple life was healthier than an affluent one and her body seemed to confirm this. She was rarely sick.

But she hadn't been raised to sacrifice. Tessa could not forget her family's Friday night trips to the bank, a high-ceilinged granite sanctuary on Main Street of their Connecticut town. Female clerks were cloistered behind metal grates where they took in and gave out money. An enormous steel door led to *the vault*. While she and her mother waited on a bench in the lobby, her father disappeared into that sanctum to do something essential and secret.

Her mother considered money one of the great unmentionables like sex and religion. Tessa knew her father kept a stack of twenty dollar bills in *the strong box* that locked with a key like a tiny version of the bank vault door. The box was kept on the floor of their bedroom closet. The bills were for Tessa's mother but all that changed when her father left and Tessa's mother discovered that he had used their savings to feed his race track habit. She was forced to sell their house and move into a one-room apartment near the highway.

"How will he support you?" she asked when Tessa announced a decade later that she was marrying David. "Don't expect anything from me."

Tessa ignored her mother's apprehension. David could find work in a library and she would start a band. David's friend

Jasper had asked them to join his commune in Vermont which was nearly free. She wouldn't be dragged down like her mother who became hysterical if her checkbook didn't balance. Why waste time balancing a checkbook when the bank sent a statement every month. Because he was good at numbers, David took care of the financial stuff.

"*Safe deposit* box is a misnomer," Tessa muttered. "Disaster dump is more like it." She and Jasper had finished at the bank and moved across Main Street to the Sap Bucket.

"But here's the good thing," Jasper said. "You weren't a signatory on his credit cards, so you're not liable."

Who is? Tessa did not ask. She stared at her Blunt Screwdriver. Jasper slugged down his shot and followed it with a sluice of beer.

"He blindsided me."

"Don't worry—"

"How can I not?" Tessa glared. "I'm in shock. There's not enough to pay the land taxes."

"How about a tequila?" Jasper ordered another lager. Tessa ignored him.

"I trusted him."

Jasper tried to look sympathetic: clenched eyebrows, weak smile. Not for the first time he marveled at the lady's powers of self-delusion. The more furtive David became, the more she'd praise his fidelity. "David doesn't even flirt," she told Jasper at a party as he glimpsed his friend hook fingers under the back of a young woman's belt.

"If they start phoning you—" Jasper began.

"Who?"

"Citi, Visa—"

"But you've already said I'm not liable so why—"

"Sometimes they try—"

"I'll never give up the farm."

"That you won't." Jasper thought of her derelict buildings, the flames visible through the cracked brick of her chimney flue.

"As long as I can pay the mortgage." Tessa took a slug of her drink. "And the back taxes."

Last year they'd been on the delinquent tax list but David reassured her he was investing what he hadn't paid in a special account to double his interest.

"He lied. He shouldn't have done that to me." Tessa swirled the pulp in her orange juice.

"But he did."

Tessa burst into tears.

"The town clerk has repayment options." Jasper came over to Tessa's side of the booth, put his arm around her. "You're not the first person—"

"To have my house auctioned off." She got up and stalked to the ladies' room.

They'd always lived on the edge and David's carefree attitude about money should have alarmed her; instead she imagined a phony firewall. She found for a pen in her purse and unfurled toilet paper:

I love you so
My all in all
You pick me up
Before I fall
No need to make

A booty call
I'm in your bed already.
Safe haven, you,
From free for alls
For wealth and fame
The games I botch
Seem not to bother you at all
My darling firewall.

She came out of the stall, splashed water on her face, then took off her snood, coiled her tousled hair into a knot, stretched, replaced the snood, then fiddled with tendrils of hair to soften the effect.

"What's with the hairnet?" Jim Dawson watched Tessa approach. He usually stopped by the Sap after a house closing.

"Shh." Jasper lowered his voice. "Husband just died. Great guy."

Tessa sat down, pushed away her orange drink. "I think I'd like to go." She looked with indifference at an apparent acquaintance of Jasper's.

"Oh, pardon me!" Jasper introduced Tessa to Jim. "Harriet Dawson's son."

Tessa nodded, smiled. "She's a lovely person." *Not like you.* Darting blue eyes and thinning hair that held the remains of what may have been henna dye.

"One of Harriet's biggest fans was our pal Rory," Jasper added.

"That little salami slammer?" Jim sipped vodka.

Tessa tightened her mouth and looked away in savage disregard. "North Haven doesn't suffer homophobes lightly."

Jim let out a honk of laughter. "Just kidding, Rory's great."

"I'm ready to go." Tessa gathered up her pocket book.

"Just let us finish up." Jasper smiled desperately. "Jim's a crackerjack realtor."

Tessa said nothing.

"He's thinking of leaving us for the greener parking lots of the south but I'm trying to show him how much we have to offer here."

Don't bother.

Jim stared at something behind her and Tessa reflexively turned to see three girls sitting around a pitcher of beer.

Always eyeballing the babes. Poor Harriet. How did she produce such a son? A moderate pot beneath his pale blue shirt and regimental tie, so like David's clothes. Tessa remembered Harriet's house on Sand Hill Rd. She felt herself entering a fog, drifting, as Jasper made a show of arranging David's probate files while Jim continued a running patter of jokes at his own expense about how he had no friends around here while his mother was a local celebrity. "—could hold my funeral in a phone booth and still have room."

"Tessa's got a sweet old place up on Hyssop Road," Jasper interjected. "She's in a transition with it and maybe you could give her the benefit of your experience."

"In what?" Tessa stared at Jim.

"Real estate." Make me feel like a bug why don't you, Jim thought. A broad with a bad attitude. Must be a byproduct of rural life.

"I'm not planning to sell." Tessa stood up.

"No, but hang on Tess." Jasper turned to Jim. "Tessa's interested in generating some rental income."

"You've got apartments?" Jim asked.

"I'm not a landlady," Tessa stepped out of the booth.

"Maybe Jim could help you troubleshoot," Jasper followed her.

"I'm not anticipating more *trouble* and I don't *shoot*." Hearing Tessa's reply, the three girls laughed.

"She's good, isn't she!" Jim said to the girls. More laughter.

Tessa moved toward the door.

"Jim could help you with an upgrade—"

"I'm not upgrading, "Tessa said over her shoulder.

"He's a wizard at bringing people and houses together. Right bro?" Jasper grinned.

Jim watched Tessa ignore him in favor of her pocket book. He'd really like to take a pass on this lady.

"He sees the potential," Jasper persisted.

"I know what I've got." Tessa was through the door.

"No, but really, he'll bring a fresh eye." Jasper caught the door and stood aside for Jim.

Tessa cast a weary eye at her old friend. "I need to get home."

That evening, in front of the wood stove, Tessa unrolled the toilet paper from her bag, copied the lyrics into a notebook, and kept going.

You slay me with your eyes, your mouth
Your necktie waves bye bye.
My disappearing safety net
Your graceful exit
Side-steps debt.

And now the room grows fearful hot
I'm singed by all that you are not:
Alive, for one thing
Solvent, another
An able fix for all my trouble.

15

The Hutch

Carless in the rain: how could this be? Melissa was how. Since her baby was born, she'd got all militant, wouldn't let her mother drive three minutes to the motel to pick up her cleaning gear. *Mom, you aren't legal!* Why not scream it from the rooftops? After she and Kim were evicted and Melissa was moving back in with her father, she was like *Mom, you aren't allowed on the premises* when the restraining order expires in how many days?

It had always been this way. Nothing worked because everybody was out for themselves. Kim's own mother putting Benadryl in their bottles to shut them up while she watched football. No wonder they were all ADHD before people knew what that was. Nobody could sit still long enough to finish high school. And now Melissa only thinking of how to cause Kim pain.

She dug out her phone, called Bill, got the answering machine.

"I just need to pick up my hutch." Then she called her daughter.

"Your dad says it's okay. I'm in the bus shelter on Coolidge by the dollar store."

She put away her phone, glanced at the others. A black guy she recognized from around town. A super-sized guy in an electric wheelchair, a well-known drunk with a face on fire.

Someone splashed down the street and into the shelter, began shaking rain off.

"Move down the end if you wanta do that. Please." The wheelchair guy smiled on the last word.

"I'm cool with that." The new guy moved away, pulled back his rain hood and slicked his hair with both hands. Kim didn't recognize him. Kind of cute.

She put down her tote and felt for cigarettes. The man held one out and everybody watched as she felt for her lighter and he lighted hers from his own.

"Well, thanks," she murmured.

"No problem." He smiled. "How far to the highway?"

Everyone turned at the sound of a muffler. An old Mercedes pulled up to the curb.

Kim picked up her tote, motioned to him. "We'll drop you there." She opened the back door.

"No cigarettes in here!" Melissa yelled from the front seat.

Kim stubbed her butt and put it in her pocket. "Scoot in." She pressed against the baby's car seat and made room for the man.

"I'm not taking strangers." Melissa recognized that look in her mother's eyes—hyper alert, like Gran's when she gambled, only this was about guys.

"He's just going to the onramp on 91."

"Oooh, that's a cute baby." The man reached across Kim and jiggled the baby's car seat.

Melissa glared in the rear view. "I need him to sleep."

"Sorry." The man pulled back his hand, raised his eyebrows at Kim.

Nobody said anything. They jounced through pot holes, past a mini-mall, gas stations. Melissa pulled over beneath the highway overpass and the man opened the door.

"Thanks," he said. "Be good."

"No better 'n you," Kim said.

He shut the door.

Melissa let out a rasping sigh.

Kim snorted. "Well I'm sorry you feel that way."

Melissa shifted into low gear and the car bucked, backfired, and started an uphill climb between woods. Her phone rang.

"Hey." She glanced at the back seat. "You know I got Mom with me."

"Calm down, Bill," Kim raised her voice. "Just give me the hutch and I'll leave."

"If you wake up Douglas, I'll kill you." Melissa clicked off. "You got bigger things to worry about than a hutch."

"Don't start." Kim had owned her mistakes: the overdrinking and the guys, the threatening behavior, the DUI. Losing her cleaning job was not her fault. The motel owner accused her of stealing a jewelry bag, if anyone in that dump even had jewelry, which she highly doubted.

"I got him to care for fulltime." Melissa interrupted her thoughts and for a moment Kim thought she was talking about Bill.

"I didn't say I wouldn't help you with the baby. I just need the one heirloom that's mine."

"You are the last person I want help from." Melissa turned onto a dirt road. At a mailbox she swung up a muddy driveway.

"Somebody stole my planter." Kim pointed.

Melissa was silent as she jostled the car over ruts.

"They don't make lavender toilets any more. Remember the purple petunias I had in it?"

Silence.

"It was in the Saturday paper."

The car headlights showed up a flat-bed truck, a snowmobile, a line of overflowing trashcans and a gas grill in front of a one-story house. Behind it stood a slab wood shed and a paddock.

Melissa parked next to the truck. A light went on by the front door and a man in a blue hospital gown came out on the step. Kim stared. Bill must have gained another fifty since she saw him at their court date. She followed Melissa up the steps.

"I shouldn't be out here. Getting over something." Bill looked down at the car seat. "Oh, little fella." He bent to grasp the car seat and the gown fell open.

"Cover your meat, Bill." Kim stopped a laugh.

"Cover your mouth." He picked up the car seat.

Kim pulled the door shut behind her and watched Bill walk unsteadily to his recliner and set down the baby. He was breathing heavily.

"Dad—" Melissa put her hand on her father's back.

"I'm okay." He lowered himself into the recliner. Melissa laid the baby in his lap.

Bill settled the baby in the crook of his arm. "Now we're all set. You got a bottle for him?"

Kim went to Melissa's kit bag.

"Hey!" Melissa grabbed the bottle from her mother. "You're so off limits."

"It's okay." Bill smiled down at the baby. "She's just being grandma."

"I don't believe you're letting her stay here after—"

"She's not staying." He never took his eyes off his grandson.

Kim looked around. All the unfinished stuff was still unfinished: subfloor in the kitchen, unpainted sheetrock; but now a layer of dust made the air grey. The hutch loomed against one wall. It was dirty and dark like everything else but that would change once she got it somewhere with clean windows and a real floor and not these scraps of carpet ends. The sink was full of dishes, the counter hidden beneath stacks of junk mail, pill bottles, and god knows what. She rooted under the sink, found a sponge and began washing dishes. Melissa was on the phone in the bedroom and Bill was talking to the baby. Kim scraped slime off the drain rack, found the dregs of her old bleach bottle and poured a slug on the sponge and rinsed it, then went to work on the counter, stacking, organizing, putting food away.

Melissa came out of the bedroom. "What are you doing?"

"What does it look like?"

Bill held the baby up. "Somebody needs a diaper."

"I'm just clearing some space for you." Kim put cereal boxes in a cupboard. "You got a case of soup in here."

"From the Food Shelf. It's old." Bill rubbed one bare foot. "Take it. I can't eat tomatoes."

Kim got a grip on three cans, popped the lids, poured them into a pot.

The recliner squeaked as he tried to get up. Kim went to help. "My God Bill, your foot."

"It's time for my pills." He pointed to the counter.

Kim came back with a glass of water and the pill bottle.

"I don't believe this is happening." Melissa took the baby into the bedroom.

"We all need help right now." Kim lowered her voice. "I got nowhere to go tonight, Bill."

He looked her in the eye for the first time. "There's the shed. That's it. When the nurse comes tomorrow, I'll ask her if she's heard of anything. She's good like that."

Kim knew he didn't owe her any favors but she couldn't bring herself to thank him. "I'll pick up the hutch soon as I can find somebody to help me."

"Hey, Liss!" Bill called his daughter. "Get that sleeping bag out of the closet, will you?"

Kim stood on the back step with a mug of soup. It was warm for November. The rain had stopped and a blur of moonlight showed through the clouds. So this was where she was at. She stared at the woods, the shed where her horse, Lefty, had lived. She finished the soup and walked around the house. The paint was nearly peeled off the clapboards. The bathroom window glass was out, filled with a square of insulation. Loose tarpaper dangled from the sills. The little spruce she'd put lights on each Christmas had disappeared. Probably got run over. She couldn't even find a stump. The place looked like worry had rained down on it, washing away all her touches of hope. And what nearly made her cry was that she wanted to move back in.

Melissa opened the door and threw a sleeping bag in her direction and slammed the door.

Rage swamped Kim's sadness. She should smack that bitch but she wouldn't take the bait. She began her anger management breathing, looked for something calming to stare at. She walked up to the side window where she could see the hutch. Don't change the paint Grandpa said, that's antique paint, so she left it grey with streaks of red showing through.

Kim went to the shed. The fragrance of horse manure raised her tears. She found part of a hay bale and mounded the hay beneath the window and spread the sleeping bag on top, then began searching the cracks in the wall boards where she used to stash butts. Her fingers spidered along until she felt a nubbin of happiness. She dug out matches and stood in the doorway smoking, feeling like a human being again. It'd be a long night but she was tired, she'd sleep through. In the morning she'd move the hutch into the shed and clean it up. She didn't know how Bill was going to make it. They were crazy not to accept her help but maybe it was for the best. She had enough on her plate except food. Her stomach growled. She hadn't been this thin since high school. She took a last drag on the cigarette and flicked the spark high into the air.

16

The Tenant

Tessa sat on the back step looking up the hill at the graveyard. She imagined herself seen from above by David's ghost. She looked like a garden sculpture, one of those heavily draped, pensive Victorian figures with anthropomorphized names: Remorse; Reflection; Melancholy. She hadn't changed her clothes in weeks, just added to them. She wore a camisole David had given her with a pair of his boxer shorts over her long underwear and his smallest pair of trousers. Today she'd chosen one of his argyle cardigans. Wisps of her pale hair escaped through the crochet holes of her snood. She'd slung Bessie's old dog bed around her shoulders.

Bessie had lived to be nearly twenty, and at the end, Tessa let her sleep on a disintegrating muskrat cape worn by Tessa's mother on her honeymoon to the White Mountains with Tessa's father, the cigar salesman who went to Havana and never came back. She mourned and vilified her disappeared husband until she died and insisted that Tessa resembled him with her dark eyes in dramatic contrast with her blond hair. She and Tessa spent weekends with her maternal grandmother who never stopped keening about her-son in-law's betrayal. At seventeen, Tessa fled to college, dropped out, met David and moved as far as they had gas for which turned out to be rural New England. The muskrat cape had been part of her trousseau.

Don't make any changes for a year. But her friends didn't mean that she should sink into inertia. They still checked in and brought food. She told her band she wasn't ready for gigs. Her daughter visited on weekends but found her mother so distracted by her own thoughts that she began phoning instead. The library was sending Tessa David's modest pension. She couldn't bring herself to work out a yearly budget but she knew there wouldn't be enough. In the meantime, she was not discontented with freezer burned hamburger, brown rice and the last of the kale drooping in the garden.

Clouds were lowering and the temperature, though unseasonably warm, was dropping. She longed for snow, even sleet, to provide motion. She exhaled a shroud of vapor and, in response to nothing in particular, glanced over her shoulder. A figure stood out by the mailbox. Boy or girl, man or woman, Tessa could not tell. A hoody obscured the face. It wasn't shaped like David, the legs were too long.

Tessa's hand levitated upwards. She gave a stately wave, a queen on valium. The figure approached, hands in pockets. As Tessa stood up, her snood caught in the thorns of a climbing rose. She bent to untangle the snarl and the muskrat cape slid forward, blocking her view.

A woman's hands, grey with old dirt, came to help.

"Try this." Ochre finger tips spread the knotted hair on one palm and stroked it with a thumb, slowly freeing it, strand by strand, from the thorns. Tessa smelled tobacco.

"There ya go." The woman pushed back her hoody.

Tessa took in her red hair, her cocked eyebrow and foxy smile that belied the raccoon circles beneath her eyes.

"Hey, I've seen you singing at the Waybridge Inn. You're good!"

"That was in another life." Tessa felt a smile coming on. She glanced down at the woman's filthy runners, her dirty white painter's pants and oversized wind breaker with the name of a paving company on the pocket.

"What's that smell? Better not be me." The woman laughed into a cigarette cough.

"You smoke."

"Yeah but that ain't it." The woman looked around as if the source would be among the dead weeds.

"I haven't smoked in years," Tessa said. No point in making an enemy she hadn't even met.

The woman chuckled. "Yeah, I keep quitting, too. Thing is, I'm only one cigarette away from two packs a day." Her laugh broke down into a cough.

Tessa thought she saw something furtive in her expression.

"I just lost my house and I heard you were renting rooms."

"My husband died."

"I'm sorry." She set a hand on Tessa's arm. "I really am."

Tessa was silent. The woman glanced at the front of the house where a wisteria vine had gained entrance to a bedroom window.

"I can take care of that for you!" She leaped like a basketball player, grabbed the vine and hung with it, her windbreaker scraping against the clapboards before the vine snapped.

"Nooooo!" Tessa screamed.

The woman stared at Tessa and then at the scrap of vine in her hand as Tessa wept and apologized and talked about David's love for the wisteria. The woman put her arm around her saying, *no harm done, you can't kill these things, not to worry,* all the while checking out the dooryard.

"Yo!" She eyeballed the old Ford tractor. "My grand dad taught me how to drive one of those. Does it run?"

Tessa looked Kim in the eye. "Why don't we talk about that over tea."

17

The Stern

Eliot couldn't remember how he got from the boat to the airport. The flight home was a blur and now he was traveling north by train. Josh's belongings he had consigned to a homeless shelter run by Spanish monks. Somewhere in Gibraltar, a destitute man was wearing an aquamarine cashmere tee shirt. Eliot stared out the window at the back of towns, strip malls, parking lots, lines of storage bunkers, woods, harvested fields. When the train came to the lowland slopes of the Green Mountains he felt his mouth go dry. His breath came in gasps. He must find a taxi, return to their beloved house, now sold, and retrieve the Morris Mini, his last remaining possession.

A few hours later, Eliot exited his therapist's office into late autumn sunshine. He had spent some of his last thousand dollars to have this man urge him to stay close to his feelings and reach out to his friends and, if he was having suicidal ideations, to contact a prescribing psychiatrist whose card Eliot held. He hadn't had the guts to tell the shrink that he was destitute. Twilight was bringing magenta streaks to the west. He wasn't sure he could endure twilight.

He drove down Main Street out of town past scattered commerce, a trailer park, a diner. He pulled over at the edge of woodland near a motel built when motels were called tourist cabins, now a relic, a last resort that rented weekly, monthly. A boy stood in front of one cabin. Smoke leaked from the edges of a gas grill. A man appeared. He lifted the cover on the grill, prodded, closed the lid. He said something and the boy disappeared inside and returned with a can which the man took before the boy could hand it to him. Maybe there was a woman in there, a baby. These could be Eliot's new neighbors.

* * *

To celebrate their moving Phil's mother into assisted living, Rory and Phil planned a weekend in Paris; but the night before their flight, Phil slipped on a throw rug and fractured his tibia. "I told you that would happen," Rory said. Phil was in a rug-making group. At sixty-five, he was in superior health, with excellent muscle mass and bone density and reflexes, not to mention balance. The doctor said he was to keep his foot raised and that travel was out for three weeks. So here he was seated with his boot cast up on the kitchen table.

Phil stared out the window at the garden he wouldn't be able to put to bed this fall, at the shed he'd hoped to shingle, at the empty chicken coop. The coop had been Rory's fancy but he'd lost interest. The pig pen fence needed repair now that Sweet and Sour were off at the butchers. How many more years would he have the energy to raise their own meat and freeze produce, make jam. Rory loved to offer food from 'our farm' to guests but limited himself to inside chores. Without these seasonal rituals what was to keep them from a condo in Florida?

His leg was throbbing to the beat of his heart. The throw rug had been a watershed moment.

Rory glanced at him. "You're sad. Don't be sad. Here." He handed Phil a colander of beans. "Get snappin'!"

Rory turned back to the cutting board where he was pounding chicken breasts with a wooden mallet. "Once I get through, you'll think it's Weiner Schnitzel." He smiled broadly at Phil and continued pounding. *You can make anything taste good if you have enough salt.* Rory learned these words from his mother who fed a family of six on twenty dollars a week and he had her tuna squiggle recipe as evidence.

In spite of Rory's urban ways, it was he who had brought them here from Boston, who became a fixture in the community, running the library book groups, starting the first gay men's pot luck tea dances back when there wasn't a gay bar within fifty miles. Rory did freelance editing from home and he argued they could just as easily do it in a beautiful house in the woods as in a cramped duplex in Somerville. Phil taught economics at an undistinguished college until his asthma got so bad that he couldn't lecture and took a leave. The move to North Haven felt to him like the cessation of pain. He found work in a tree nursery and took a master gardening course at night. He lived in a beautiful place, he loved his work and he had Rory, his bright star. Twenty years later, Rory still buoyed him. Their financial health wasn't as strong as Rory would wish but they still might inherit a bit from Phil's mother if her investments didn't all go to her fancy assisted living. Phil let Rory worry about the future. Things would work out.

Phil's phone chimed. Eliot and Josh had cut short their world cruise. Could they snag a dinner invitation? Like everyone, Phil and Rory were shocked that Josh's cancer had been found so late. And now here was Eliot on the phone saying 'fabulous, couldn't be better,' when Phil asked how they were.

"Probably overcompensating." Rory squinted at a wine label. "I just hope Josh isn't too far gone."

Phil didn't reply.

"Or maybe they ran out of money and had to come home." Everyone wondered how Josh and Eliot had afforded the trip. "God, I hope they don't ask us for any." Rory made his mock horror face.

"I think they know enough not to."

After the '08 crash, Josh and Eliot turned their Victorian painted lady into a B&B which must have helped, but that was before Josh got sick and nobody knew how they were managing now.

"Their finances are really none of our business." Rory poured himself a glass of wine.

"Although you love to speculate about it," Phil said. "Money, the last great mystery after sex."

"But you don't mean *our* sex." Rory advanced on his husband with a glass of wine but Phil waved it away. "You're just feeling testy because of your leg." Rory kissed the top of Phil's head and returned to a safe topic, Eliot and Josh's cruise. He couldn't imagine how they'd survived being cooped up on a ship, no matter how luxurious, for all those weeks. Phil and Rory had sailed to Antarctica and the Galapagos but these were what Rory called 'targeted experiences' that left them with a jewel box of images. A world cruise would be a hectic memory dump, no grander than an oldster's European bus tour.

That evening, Rory opened the door and stared in amazement at his friend. So thin and pale. And the navy polo shirt with the white collar was so '90s, as were the pleated trousers with—dear Lord—cuffs. And black runners?

"Where did you get those clothes?"

"Oh, you know how it is after a voyage. Everything's dirty so I found something from the back of my closet."

Rory kissed Eliot on both cheeks, ran his hand over Eliot's bleached brush cut. At least he hadn't let his hair go. But where was Josh?

"He just popped over to Walpole," Eliot said. "The wine we've been tracking has finally arrived."

"For God's sake, that's an hour away!" Rory shouted.

He and Phil exchanged puzzled glances. They went to the living room where Phil lowered himself onto the couch and propped his foot on the coffee table.

"What happened?" Eliot pointed at the cast.

"Did he trip or was he pushed?" Rory inserted.

"*Why* would you say such a thing?" Eliot asked.

"Joke!" Phil raised a cheek to accept Eliot's kiss. "I took a stupid fall. Now detail us about your trip."

For the next hour Eliot took them on a breathless chronicle of the world viewed from a deluxe two-story stateroom, through which passed beautiful, amusing people of all ages. The menus and midnight martinis were one thing, the ports were another. In Tenerife, workers drove beggars out of their path with leaf blowers, but in Melbourne they met the most gorgeous Maori boy who tattooed the bottoms of their feet. They adored the shipboard lectures on the history of high seas travel and the mysteries of the deep, and tours of temples and palace ruins—not new war ruins but ancient ones and amazingly safe.

Phil glanced at his watch.

"Where is he?"

Eliot's kept talking. After a beach breakfast at dawn on an uninhabited island off—was it Java?—he veered back to Cape Horn where the waves looked like Niagara Falls. "And Hong Kong—" Eliot widened his eyes, stared at the ceiling fan. "The sushi was supernatural and the most exquisite water gardens in spite of—"

Rory handed him a Kleenex and Eliot wiped his eyes.

"—drones in the air and junks in the sea and all those painful looking needle-nosed buildings." His laughter broke into sobs. "And the flying fish and those outriggers—no, that was another ocean."

Rory put his arm around his friend. "What's going on?"

Eliot put his head down.

"Look at me." Phil leaned forward. "You're not making sense."

"I can't," he whispered. "I shouldn't be alive."

"I'm turning everything off." Rory went to the kitchen. When he came back, Eliot was sobbing against Phil's chest.

"Josh won't be here," Phil said quietly.

"What?" Rory imagined scenarios: Josh off on a fling, or fading in some tropical hospice, or filing for divorce.

"Get the Ativan," Phil commanded Rory. When Eliot had taken a pill, he sat back and breathed deeply. "You must tell no one what I'm about to say." He stared at his hands, turned his wedding ring. "We gave up all our worldly goods for this trip except my car about which we had a terrible fight—oh, why did I refuse to sell it? I must have known." He closed his eyes, shaking.

"Breathe," Phil said.

"We cashed in my IRAs, even sold Josh's grandfather's coin collection and you know how he felt about his collections. It didn't matter because we weren't coming back."

"I'm getting more wine." Rory stood up.

Not coming back. Nothing like Josh and Eliot for melodrama, Rory thought as he brought down a bottle of Sauvignon Blanc. The hysteria over imagined betrayals and the passionate reconciliations. The hypersensitive need to know each other's whereabouts at all times. But this pact to flee their creditors seemed uncharacteristic, given Eliot's obsession with financial security and Josh's materialism.

When Rory returned, Eliot held his finger up. He would impart.

"Something you don't know: after our wedding we swore we'd never be separated. We put it in writing, had it notarized."

"That's nice." Rory glanced at Phil. "Maybe we should do that."

"We already have," Phil said. "It was in our vows."

"But somewhere at sea I changed." Eliot said.

"A sea change," Rory whispered.

Phil glared at him.

"In Hong Kong Josh bought me a cashmere bathrobe and I thought, 'Don't! I'll need that money!' I could barely eat. I stopped sleeping. I'd go on deck and walk all night thinking about how these were the last days of my life. Of our lives."

"How impossible," Rory whispered.

"We didn't know what day, but it had to be at night from the stern."

"Like Hart Crane," Rory said. He ignored Phil's glare and poured wine, held out glasses.

Eliot sipped, blew his nose, continued. "We enter the Mediterranean and it's time." He picked up his wine glass, put it down. "The first night beyond Suez, the moon rises, we prepare ourselves with champagne and Xanax. Then the sea gets rough. Terrifying waves. The stewards make us lock our terrace doors, shelter in place. So we're sitting on the floor and you know we had the best view and the worst stability on the entire ship. In a storm you want low, you want amidships, you want cheap. We had the opposite. The boat is bucking and flapping, rearing up and crashing down and I'm actually hoping it'll stay like this so we can't make our move." He groped for a tissue, blew. "Not Josh. He had such resolve."

Rory looked at Phil in alarm. Nobody spoke.

"Somehow, we needed to get down to the lowest deck and out to stern. To gain access to the sea, if you understand. And just as suddenly as the storm blew in, it faded. When the moon appeared, I felt betrayed."

"Betrayed by the moon? Why?"

"Haven't you been listening?" Eliot hissed at Rory. "So we

get ourselves cleaned up—we're in tuxedos you understand—as if we're going to dinner, which we would not be doing. We grope our way to the elevator. I'm beside myself with terror. I keep hoping someone will stop us but everybody's rushed off to the dining rooms."

Rory leaned over Eliot to grip Phil's hand. With his free hand, Phil held Eliot's wrist.

"So we're at the stern and Josh grabs me, drags me to the side and climbs on top of some brass thing that they keep hoses in—even as weak as he was he could still move like a cat." Eliot paused, drank from his glass. "What a coward I am."

"You were affirming life." Rory said.

"I was affirming fear. Which I'm beginning to think is the strongest life force." He paused.

"I would have done the same thing," Phil said. He let go of Eliot's wrist and sat back.

"For the first time in our lives we're in a physical fight, a grotesque tug of war with me trying to pull him back on deck. His grip is so tight he's about to break my wrist and, I can't stop myself, I scream for help and he lets go of me and pitches backward over the side. Just like that." Eliot clapped his hands. "Josh. Gone. I didn't hear the splash." He shut his eyes. "No trace of him. Just ocean and moonlight."

"Tragic and beautiful," whispered Rory.

"Shut up," said Phil.

Rory looked on the verge of tears. "Why did you say that?"

"I don't want you to take over. It's Eliot's story."

"I was just repeating what he said. I was honoring his words."

They sat for a while in silence. Phil turned to Eliot. "I don't want to seem crass but you should eat something."

During chicken piccata, Eliot continued.

"A woman runs out on deck. She'd seen it all from her stateroom and she calls the doctor as if that would help. The captain comes down and there's the most tremendous hub-bub. Then all the legal stuff. Amazing how these boats are prepared for everything." He looked at his hosts. "I'm alive and I have nothing."

"Like the majority of the world's population, "said Phil.

"Don't!" Rory glared at Phil. He turned to Eliot. "It's instinct! You wanted to live."

"But how?" Eliot ran one hand over his stomach. "I'm a destitute, fat, old queen."

"You're not fat!" Rory laughed.

"You can't imagine my situation, can you? You think 'Oh, he's exaggerating the way he does' but I assure you it's a fact. I'm looking for something minimum wage, just to put gas in the car, just to have a bit of food. It feels like another form of death, a kind of void."

"I can't take it in." Rory spread his arms. "Josh is at the bottom of the ocean with—"

"Stop!" Eliot cried.

"Why didn't you tell us right away when you called?" Phil's voice was strained.

"What difference does it make now?" Eliot shouted.

Phil came around the table to sit beside him.

"The truth is—" Eliot paused. "The truth is that the past feels realer than the present."

Nobody spoke.

"It seems...inadmissible that I should have plunged myself into poverty and homelessness. You know I was just out at the Candlestick."

"That place?" Phil exclaimed. "I thought they closed."

"Well pardon me but I have nowhere to live."

"We can't have that!" Rory looked at Phil. "We can't have Eliot at the Stick." He turned to his friend. "Stay here."

While Eliot went to collect his belongings, Phil watched Rory clean the kitchen. "I cannot understand why he ever agreed to it."

"You're so reasonable." Rory slugged down the remains of Phil's wine and put the glass in the dishwasher. "You couldn't grasp their kind of love."

"And you can."

Rory turned on the dishwasher. "But I've never experienced it because I live with you!"

"Which means?"

"If I was dying you'd be googling my replacement." Rory leaned down and chucked Phil under the chin. "I've always known this about you. It's part of what fascinated me. The way you were always holding something in reserve."

"You're drunk and I'm going outside." Phil stood up and reached for his cane.

"You're not to walk!" Rory rushed forward. "The ground is uneven, you might trip."

Phil opened the sliding door.

"I don't like what you're doing!" Rory turned on the outside light. As he watched his husband limp downhill, he imagined that he was seeing him for the last time. Rory adjusted his reflection in the window so he could see his three-quarter profile, his best aspect. He was still attractive. He doubted he would attract anyone as beautiful as Phil but it hardly mattered since this was fantasy and in real life Rory would die first. He peered outside, trying to see beyond the circle of light. Eventually he made out Phil's pale sweater approaching.

"I'm sorry." Rory called.

"No, you're not." Phil came inside and filled a glass of water at the sink. "This is you wanting a little drunken spat because it's easier than sex. It makes you feel alive."

"Oh, don't insult our sex life!" Rory wailed. "And I *do* want to apologize. And please get your weight off that foot."

Phil ignored him and limped to the bathroom. Rory went upstairs to prepare the guest room. After Eliot returned and was settled for the night, Rory helped Phil into bed, arranged his foot on pillows, and brought him a cup of mint tea. When they were both in bed, Phil did not rebuff Rory when he drew close.

"I still don't understand that 'shut up' business," Rory said.

"Okay, it wasn't nice. I just wanted you to calm down."

"If you get sick it reassures me to know that you won't expect me to kill myself."

Phil snorted.

As he lay with his head on Phil's shoulder, Rory talked about how important it was to be grateful for each day and how blessed they were to have each other and enough money and their health.

"We're responsible people," Rory whispered. "Not like the ones who hang out their test results on Facebook asking for everybody's opinion, as if you can crowdsource your treatment. Whatever happened to privacy?"

"Who puts their tests on Facebook?" Phil wanted to know.

"Actually, I heard that Josh did. Or maybe Eliot did it for him. That's how everybody knew he was terminal."

"Well, it's irrelevant now." Phil said. He sighed in a way that indicated the subject was closed. They lay quietly.

"What Eliot faces is no joke."

"Of course, it's awful," Rory said. "I'm glad we're helping but we can't do everything."

"Nobody's asking us to." Phil's eyes were closed.

"But they might."

"Now you're sounding like Eliot."

"How do I sound like Eliot?" Rory raised his voice to a whispered hiss.

"Fear."

"I'm not frightened. I'm just a responsible person speaking the truth. There's a limit to what we can do. My God, we just finished with you mother."

Phil shifted his leg.

"You know how on planes they tell you to put the oxygen mask on yourself before you help anyone else?" Rory continued. "That's all I'm saying."

Rory hit the water backwards, his face to the sky. He plunged, rose to the surface, gasped for air. The ship was a glittering monster spewing foam as it receded. He swallowed water, choking, crying out, then sinking with eyes and mouth open. How long until he suffocated?

The bedroom door creaked. Rory jerked awake.

"Please forgive me," Eliot was shaking. "I cannot sleep."

Rory sat up. "I've been having the most ghastly dream."

"Who?"

Rory was shocked to hear Phil who usually slept like a hibernating bear.

Eliot came closer until he was looking down at his friends in their big bed. There were sweat stains under the arms of his t-shirt.

"I'm so frightened," Eliot quavered. "Just tonight. Just so I can feel I'm back in a world I know. Could I share your bed?"

"Get in on the other side." Phil yawned. " I've got this leg to deal with."

"Oh, yes, of course, I forgot." Eliot came to Rory.

"We love our king," Rory said.

"I appreciate this." Eliot slid under the duvet.

Rory wriggled around, trying to get comfortable. Why hadn't he insisted that Eliot sleep on the chaise longe in the corner? He became aware of conflicting smells. On his left was Phil's cologne, a green and gold scent he'd worn for years. From Eliot's side came a vegetative odor like rotting garbage. *The poor soul, he's traumatized.* But it was difficult for Rory to pity someone who stank. He listened to Phil's regular breathing as it turned into a soft purring snore.

Eliot tightened his abdominals and tried to flatten the sheet over his stomach but there was no smoothing out the rise of his gut compared to Rory's flatness. How absurd I am! Eliot thought, to be concerned with my appearance at a time like this. He could still recreate the feel of Josh's grip but now, he was shocked to realize, it was Rory's grasp he recalled, the way Rory danced in their club days, push/pulling Eliot into a kind of whip lash. Eliot had loved the edge of sadism in Rory's dancing. They were well partnered, their friends said, and, if they hadn't been so alike, perhaps they would have been together. Rory would deny the existence of that three-way on Eliot's living room floor— pre-Phil—whereas Eliot remembered details right down to the whorl of blond hair on the back of the boy they picked up. They were really so conservative, so easily shocked, he and Rory. But they participated. They slept with friends and strangers but nobody long term. And now here they were in bed again as a coda, an elegy, with Phil in the unlikely role of the third. Eliot had never got beyond Phil's aloofness, a quality that reminded him of Josh, but in Josh's case it was meant to cover his insecurity. Was Phil insecure and, if so, about what? Eliot did not know. He squeezed his eyes shut. It was vital that he not think about Josh. Now that he'd chosen to survive, he must trust in the universe just as Josh had urged him to do as he prepared to plunge out of life.

If Rory had earplugs he could block out Eliot's tiny piercing snore, like a car alarm. Perhaps he could move to the chaise longe or the guest room. No, he'd be damned if he'd be driven out of his own bed. So much of the world's population slept in unpleasant ways, as Phil would say. He closed his eyes and tried to calm his mind. He'd never felt close to Josh and he did not miss him now. Eliot had been loyal to Josh until he couldn't and then Josh let go. They each must have known there are limits to what we can do for each other.

18

Foxy

Bill wasn't even through the door and the saleswoman was on him. Hi, how are you? Good. In dark blue sweat pants and hoodie, he thought he looked way less than 300 pounds.

"Can I help you find anything?" She put down a stack of panties. Buy two get one free. Chinese crap.

He sucked on his water bottle. "Where's the shapewear?" He was sweating. "For my wife."

"Against the back wall." She pointed.

He had to make this fast while Melissa was spending her gift coupon at the baby store.

"What size?" The woman followed him, must think he didn't know what he was doing. He knew what he was doing.

"Oh,....she's... about like me." Pawing through black lace bustiers.

"Two peas in a pod!" She gave a little laugh. "Like me and my husband."

He was deep into the lace all-in-ones.

"Let me show you something in a 2."

Easing him into plus sizes. He eyeballed the price.

"Anything more....down ticket?" He'd heard that on TV.

She was riffling a wall of beige spandex. Flapped like shower curtains. Pulled out another bustier then stopped. "Oh, you wanted the total shaper, I'm sorry!"

Amazing how some women apologized for nothing. Not his ex-wife. The saleswoman moved down a few racks He looked at his watch. Melissa was fast, he'd need to move. The saleswoman came back with black and beige and pink. He glanced at the price tag.

"Yeah, that's good. The pink one."

At the cash, he waved away a *Foxy Lady Lingerie* bag. He'd taken a decoy from the dollar store where he'd gone for a Tootsie Rolls—had to buy something.

He couldn't stop walking until he was clear of the store, couldn't let Melissa see him, but the exit looked like it was at the end of a wind tunnel, the most he'd walked in how long? He lowered himself onto a bench, wiped his face with the cuff of his hoodie. A skinny girl ran by, trying to catch her toddler. Pregnant, no less. Kim had been like that, swinging off a rope into the river when she was about to pop.

He stood up. One step at a time like the PT girl said. He yanked open the door, felt his shoulder do that popping thing but the air outside smelled good. The hot dog guy was open for the leaf peepers. He could eat three no sweat but it would interfere with the day's agenda. A deep breath sent him into a cough but he gulped it back. He walked between a couple of beaters to a sky blue Camaro with New Hampshire plates. Immaculate interior. Six forward gears. The sight of it wiped his day clean. A car like that required shelter which he did not have. He moved on to Melissa's rusted out Mercedes. She had her butt sticking out the back door as she strapped the baby in his seat.

"Soon as I drop off Dad I'll be right over." On her cell, too, multitasking.

He knew she'd move out as soon as she could but right now they needed each other. Her jerk boyfriend was not in the picture, ditto his mother, but Great Gran Charisse wanted a look at her offspring. Which gave Bill at least an hour.

* * *

"We'll be back before I run out of gas." That used to be Kim's line. "Have fun." Bill made a clucking noise at the baby, watched them jounce down the driveway.

Back in the house, he locked himself in the bathroom, pulled out the pink spandex. He lowered himself on to the toilet, landing with one cheek over the edge, grabbed the sink, then heel and toed himself out of his runners, peeled off his socks. He avoided looking at his feet as he stood up, held onto the sink while he pulled the hoodie over his head one-handed and hauled down his sweats. No underwear to mess with. He held up the shapewear and already he had an erection.

Even after swabbing himself with a towel he was still sticky. He opened the medicine cabinet. No powder. What was the other stuff? Cornstarch. In the kitchen, he rummaged through cupboards, found a box of Bisquick from Kim's pancake days. He shook some into his hand, patted it on his stomach, his crotch.

He sat back on the toilet and got one foot through the spandex, then the other. Such sweat! He pulled the spandex up to his knees. Do not eyeball the varicose. He stood up, grabbed the leg holes and dragged them to his thighs. Amazing how wide this stuff could stretch. He'd seen something on TV about how new fashion fibers were taken from the military. As close to the Army as he'd ever got. He had to sit down again, panting, sweating. More Bisquick. More tugging. He was working so hard he lost his erection.

He'd forgot the bra. Walking like a geisha, he hobbled to the bedroom closet. In the back behind a stack of insulation from the window job he'd never finished sat a metal strongbox. He pulled out the black lace brassier he'd bought on Ebay when he had an account, sniffed it. The smell of his own deodorant made him hard again. In there, too, was a pair of control top panties. He threw them back.

Back in the bathroom, he faced the mirror. Even tougher than pulling on the garment was creating the look. This bra was old school: 100% nylon lace, no spandex, no padding, and with an underwire from hell. He lifted a slab of belly fat and stuffed it into one cup, then tugged more into the other. He arched his back and a strip of fat pushed out the bottom of the bra. He jammed it back in. His legs were shaking. His penis was twisted up inside the crotch of the spandex. He'd been so rushed he forgot to curl it down between his legs. Remembering his stiff cock nearly touching his asshole made him harder. With his hands beneath the bra to keep the fat in place, he arched his back.

He looked in the mirror. This was it. The bra was full, gorgeous. His nipples were hard. Below his hands the strip of naked midriff was smoothed tight. Inside the spandex his gut and hips swelled out. He leaned over the sink for a closer view of his cleavage. As he reached his tongue down toward the slit, he felt himself coming.

"Anybody home!"

Kim's holler.

"Bill?" Closer.

"BILL?" Knocking on the bathroom door.

"Back off! I'm on the can."

Silence. Then, from farther off. "Lookit, I'm picking up the hutch."

That fucking hutch. Besides her horse, the only thing she cared about, forget being a wife or mother or grandmother.

He heard a man's voice, a thud.

"Don't scrape the floor!" Bill yelled.

He heard shuffling, her laugh.

"We're done!" she yelled. The front door slammed.

He'd lost his hard-on and he'd lost the look. He unhooked the bra, let his stomach collapse and began the downward roll of the spandex. Flour was caked in his gut creases. He'd be finding it for weeks. He couldn't bear to look at himself, sweaty hair in his eyes, dingleberries of flour on his pubic hair. Back when he was thinner Kim bought him a men's silk thong but it just made him horny for a garter belt. And he wasn't into the leather gay stuff, the S & M. He remembered running his hands up and down his mother's summer nighty when he was a kid, wanting what she had on.

"Are you gonna dress up?" Kim would say. He needed her to watch, the only audience he'd ever wanted. She got *sick of the whole thing,* said he should go out to the gay bar or go online or to the LGBT therapist in town. She did not get it. He told her *do what you want, go with other guys, just watch me sometimes is all I'm asking.* Then everything speeded up with dope and pills and Melissa calling the cops on her own mother. *It happens,* Charisse said. Some attitude for a great grandmother.

While he was here, he might as well bite the bullet, take a shower. He got one foot over the side of the tub, braced himself on the shower spigot and raised the other foot. It was easier in the hospital with all the grab bars. The visiting nurse said she'd bring a chair but since his foot healed, he didn't qualify. He let the water flow, closed his eyes, lifted his gut, sluiced water down his sides, turned to wet his back.

Out of the shower, he opened the window to let out the steam and saw, at the end of the driveway, a red truck and a guy in an EMT vest. Who was hurt? Who was dying? He squinted. Only a flagman on the road crew. Looked like Lebow. He should apply for that job, get himself outside and in shape. Kim flagged for a while after she lost some cleaning clients. She said that besides the weather and the exhaust and the standing on your feet all day it was a piece of cake.

19

Flag Man

By the time he reached the mailbox, Bill's sweatshirt was soaked but he'd walked the length of his driveway just like he'd never done with the diabetes program they gave him in the hospital. Eat fruit and vegetables, set exercise goals: walk out to the mailbox and back, then a half mile, a mile. He'd accomplished step one and his reward was Matt Lebow in a hard hat with his gut hanging out of a neon yellow vest. Bill felt a gust of lightheartedness. The guy must have gained fifty since he saw him last.

Matt is leaning on an orange Stop and Slow sign, talking to an old guy on a backhoe as another guy shoveled in the ditch. No way did Bill want to shovel. He'd stand on his feet until his varicose veins popped rather than move dirt. Maybe he recognized the digger. The younger brother of Flint, a guy Bill hated in high school, what was the kid's name? Who cares, he's not a kid now, bald under his baseball cap, glancing up and down at Bill. He cannot recall Bill. A relief.

Car coming. Bill stepped backward, almost fell in the ditch, caught himself and climbed the bank, heart pounding. Matt moved out of the way of an old Toyota and oh, shit, was that Tina? His former sister in law. "Hey!" out the window at Matt. Don't make me late for work, yuck yuck. What was she doing? Hadn't seen her in a year. She doesn't see him, wouldn't expect him here. Pretty soon he'd need to smile and flap a hand like Matt, cool, greeting the public but not hyper like Crazy Jack who likes to direct traffic at the circle as if he's the center of the universe. Amazing somebody hadn't run him over as a public service.

"How you doin'?" Matt calls up to him.

"Been worse." Bill's heart pounds in his stomach. "I got a quick question."

"If you want today's number you're too late, Eddie just won the jackpot, didn't you Ed?"

"Won jack."

I was right, Bill thinks, younger brother of that asshole Flint. Yuck yuck.

Matt looks at his watch. "Hang on. Ten minutes we go on break."

"Sure." Bill would kill for a cigarette. Already his work boots were killing him. Do not interrupt the workers.

The two guys squatted beside the backhoe with their go cups while Matt stood with Bill listening to his story: how he'd been working out of state—technically true but two years ago— and he needed something to fill in while he looked for something long term. Matt took his time to answer while Bill stared above Lebow's head at a cleared hillside and a bank of solar whatchacallits. When did that happen? They were springing up like mushrooms. *Energy for the people.* Not hardly, unless you had a trust fund.

"Matter of fact I need somebody to take over for me while I go up north. You certified?"

Oh shit. Bill shook his head.

"No problem. Watch the webinar and I'll give you the test. "

Five minutes later, Bill was walking back to the house holding a dead lottery ticket where Matt had written the address of a website. He could use a two-way radio and hold a sign, why did he need a friggin' test? Their computer hadn't worked since Kim dropped it.

"I hear they got some at the library," Melissa said, that night.

The next morning, she dropped him at the tiny North Haven Library just as Judy Adams the librarian was beginning story time. A circle of toddlers looked up at him like he was a space alien. The smell of baby powder made him queasy with excitement.

"Hey, man." A fiercely bearded father came out of the bathroom holding his son.

"Where's the computers?"

The guy pointed to a side room.

Slug that mochachino, concentrate! Optional advance cone set-ups, buffer zones, transitional zones, the number of feet legally required in a buffer zone in each speed zone, the number of cones used in a downstream taper, spaced how far apart? *Channelizing devices may be substituted for temporary longitudinal edge line pavement markings....* Say what? When would he need this crap? But he could be sued for *improper advance cone set-up* if he got it wrong and somebody had an accident. His hands stuck to the keys and he didn't like how fast his heart was beating. okay, for fuck sake: know the qualities of a successful flagger: trained, motivated, alert. He was being *trained* right now. He was *motivated* to make some money. As long as he had coffee, a water bottle and a Snickers he could stay *alert*. Make eye contact with the drivers? Who did that? Okay, whatever.

"We close in ten minutes," the librarian said.

Bill glanced around. Where had everybody gone? He'd been studying. Amazing.

That night, he couldn't sleep, cones and lane dividers kept cycling while he couldn't remember the new words that he'd listed and put under his pillow to check himself. The next morning at 6:30 he borrowed Melissa's car, got himself a large mochachino at the Quick Stop and found the road crew at the gas pump behind the General Store. Matt introduced him to Kenny and Will and the flagger, Todd, a wiry guy in his forties Bill recognized but couldn't remember from where.

Bill forgot his cheat sheet. "Just to go over the technical stuff."

"No problem," Matt squinted at his phone. "It's true/false. All you need to do is stand here and I'll ask you the questions."

The crewmen moved to the far side of the backhoe like this was punishment.

Matt held the screen at eye level. "Okay, which of these words gives you the option of doing or not doing something. You SHALL. You COULD. Or you MAY."

Fuck! What was this, an English test?

"Say that again?"

"Shall. Should. May. Which word gives you options."

Fuck! FUCK! Not 'shall' which was where you had no choice. Should do or may do. No difference. Trick question! Oh what the *fuck*."

"Should." He liked the sound of it better.

"Nope."

Bill felt his asshole quiver.

"Don't know what they were trying to prove there." Matt chuckled.

He liked Matt. Heard he'd lost a boy. Very sad.

"Try this one: where does the flagger stand: in the middle of the work lane facing traffic, on the side of the road, in the lane opposite the work."

Bill stared up at a shaft of sunlight just clearing the hill. *Help me.*

"The first one."

"Yup."

Bill paced in a circle. He was going to do this, he had to do it.

"You're good to go," Matt declared, a half hour later. "The one you didn't get—that's actually good. Perfect looks like cheating."

Bill never in his life got a perfect score.

"I'll print you the certification card and you can start tomorrow." Matt pointed to the bank below the solar collectors. "Stick around. You'll get the idea of how to do things way better than online."

* * *

"This is the last time I'm stuck here all day without a car."

Melissa held the baby slumped over her shoulder one-handed. He wasn't asleep, just staring, expressionless. He was gaining weight but Bill wondered if he was normal. Bill made a face at the kid. At 4 months shouldn't he be smiling?

Something hissed on the stove. A pot of Kraft Dinner was boiling over. "Now see what you made me do waiting for you?"

Melissa inherited Kim's blame gene. Bill turned off the stove, tried to wipe up the gluey mess.

"Is there any more of this?"

"'Don't expect me to make it for you. I got him to do." Melissa set the pot on the table, began eating. "Didn't the nurse say to watch carbs?"

"Yeah, I'm watching." And he was watching his daughter gain weight, too.

"Drop me at work tomorrow and I'll find something at Roger's after work. Matt'll take me."

"And pay with what?"

"NOT YOUR PROBLEM!" Find out what's wrong with him.

"Okay but after this I'm not driving you."

The crew had moved to Larks Hill Road. Matt was setting up cones when Bill arrived at 7:15.

"Lucky I was here," Matt said.

Bill made up something about the baby needing a diaper. Could Matt drop him at Roger's after work?

Matt stared at him like he was a bug. "I'm going up north. That's why you're here." He smiled as if Bill was the joke.

Oh yeah, well maybe one of the guys could drop him at Roger's. He'd ask.

"I'd wait 'til the end of the day."

Already fucked up. Bill put on the neon vest, picked up the sign and went to the center of the road. Trained, Alert. He forgot the third.

"Can't have anything with you. Leave it by the side of the road and save it for break. No distraction."

Yeah, of course, Bill knew that.

Almost immediately there was traffic. Todd stopped the line at his end. One car, another, another. Rush hour. The line stretched around a bend. The radio let out nonstop static. Bill kept his eye on the backhoe driver. He was the one to decide when the flagger could let the line through. That and timing. You tried not to go beyond ten minutes a side when there was a line.

"...comin' through," Todd's voice nearly drowned by noise.

A pickup piled high with hay bales passed. Bill eyeballed a girl driving and an old guy beside her. Must be some Bigelows from the farm on the ridge. A beat up Camry passes with a black guy. Unusual. A new SUV with an old couple. The last car was another Camry beater and at the wheel – he couldn't believe this – Kim. Next to her a guy in sunglasses. HEY! Kim trails her hand out the window, almost touches him. Jesus. He turns to check the license plate. Bill's head reels speculations: she's sleeping with the guy and he's given her a car; it's his car; she and this guy are working together. Off to work they go. The shit is rising around him, a cesspool of moroseness is his self esteem.

The radio squawks. *Be alert!* He turns the sign, hurries to the center of the lane and just those ten steps are making him feel like he's seventy. He has to lose weight. Stand up straight. Eye contact. He can hear the backhoe but won't look. Keep your eye on the traffic. A woman with a baby in a car seat. Fuck! It's

Melissa. She must be going to her grandmother's to drop off the kid. She gives the slightest flip of her fingers off the wheel as she passes him, eyes expressionless. In a lull, he stands so he can see Todd and watch his end too, be on top of the situation. *Motivated.* That's the word. What does that mean? Motive. A reason to do something. The motive for a murder. Hatred, greed, jealousy, anger. Bill would never kill anyone. He didn't have those motives. Most people didn't which is why that stuff was all over TV because it was rare and gross and people were curious about nasty stuff. Killer instinct meant your ability to get what you wanted, succeed. In Bill's case, probably not. Kim, on the other hand, had drawn a gun. He couldn't rule out the possibility that she'd use it. Should, may, shall. Not on her family. Not on anybody. He liked strong women. He was just bad at tests, especially tests you take standing in a parking lot. Where'd she take her test? Couldn't remember. She'd quit after a street patch job in town, went back to cleaning. Weird thing: he'd liked it when she pulled a gun on him.

"Yo!"

Caught thinking! He flipped the sign to SLOW. A line of cars—he was losing interest in making eye contact with the drivers. Sometimes someone waved. Sometimes he recognized them and it felt good that they wanted to salute him. The last car slows, a rusty Subaru station wagon with lumber tied to a roof rack.

"Hey bro!" His brother Chad leans across the front seat.

"Call you later! I need a lift after work."

He waves the next car past, the next. When the line is through, he steps back, leans on his sign while Todd is letting his line form. No one coming from Bill's side. The backhoe is on the move and it's only 10:45.

The afternoon is a death march down an open road that feeds into the state highway and traffic is up. He concentrates on breathing, keeping his toes moving. A pickup rattles by with a trailer full of mowers. His first job was raking grass and picking up pine cones when he was seven years old, while his father mowed. Bud's Lawn and Garden in stick-on letters. Bill doesn't remember any garden work. Just before everyone bought riders his dad ruined his heart going uphill with a gas push mower. On a windy day somebody's wash blew off the line. Brassieres and garter belts and girdles scattered on the grass. His father said to wash his hands at the hose and pick up the underwear to keep it from being sprayed with grass clippings, so Bill picked up a pair of lace underpants that looked like a spiderweb . He held them up to himself.

"What the fuck's matter with you?" His father swatted Bill's head.

"Get on it!" The radio squawks and he steps into the road to stop a limousine and a school bus. The afternoon goes by. On break , Bill pisses in the ditch. Farts out the grinder he brought for lunch. He tries to stomp away the prickles in his feet. Somebody yells, "Hey buddy!" Keeps him busy for a while trying to place an old red Camaro. At the end of the day, Todd says he'll see him tomorrow morning at the town garage. Bill figures Todd won't fire him until Matt returns.

* * *

Roger Leturner, the local horse trader, lives in a compound of school buses, surrounded by throngs of cars and pickups jammed into a length of dirt and weeds, hemmed in between a busy road and steep woods rising like a green wall. Chad has brought Bill here after work, to look at cars.

"She's been through a few scrapes," Roger says, of a 1990 Jaguar sedan. "Which probably totaled the other car." He chuckles. "The XJs are tough. Kid brought her in, said he got her from his grandmother. I wanted five." He opens the door to show blue leather. "She's the car of the royal family."

"Who?" Chad asked.

"She's a classic." Roger directs this at Bill. "An investment."

"Don't have the money."

"There must be stuff wrong with it or it wouldn't be here." Chad looks at Bill when he says this. *You gotta be tough. They don't call him Rotten Roger for nothing.*

"Of course there's things wrong!" Roger looks exasperated. "Something's wrong with all my cars! That's why I give deals. This is a serious deal."

"Can't afford it." Bill peered in the window of a Hyundai repainted orange. He kicks a tire, winces.

"You don't want that," Roger said. "You're worth more than that."

"If I can afford it, I want it." Bill squints at the odometer.

"Come back over here, my boy."

Bill let himself be led back to the Jaguar.

"Get in," Roger commands. "Get in and turn the key."

After hesitating the engine catches.

Bill listens to a guttural thrumming.

"That's the Jaguar purr, " says Roger. "World renowned."

"It's low," says Chad. "But it ain't no purr." He gets in the passenger side. Bill takes the car out of park—he prefers a standard shift—and nudges the gas pedal. His toe kills. The car jumps forward and comes to rest with its hood jammed under the rear bumper of an old Land Rover.

"Fuck," says Bill.

"Hang on," Chad opens his door. "We gotta lift the ass of that Rover."

Roger appears with a jack. "Get busy." He hands Bill the jack, drills the men with his eyes.

Bill cranks the jack until it hits the bumper, then he gets in the Jaguar. Chad grips the bumper with both hands. His face goes blank as if his brains have drained into his shoulder muscles. With a creak, the Land Rover bumper lifts an inch. Bill reverses the Jaguar and Chad lowers the Land Rover's bumper onto the jack.

"You guys have fucked with my two best vehicles." He looks at them.

Silence. Bill runs a thumb down a vertical crease in the Jaguar's hood while Chad examines a dent like a tiny dimple in the Rover's bumper.

"You know that, don't you? My two best vehicles."

"How 'bout $500 now and the rest at the end of the month," Bill says. "For the Jag."

Roger stares at him in mild incredulity. "And another $350 to get that Rover's fender banged out."

With a check for $250 and a loan of the same amount from Chad, Bill takes possession of the car with paperwork and a temporary license plate supplied by Roger.

"I will find you," Roger warns. "If you don't come back with that money. This ain't the Riviera. A Jag stands out around here."

20

Corn Flakes

No hand rails and no light, so Kim braced herself against the walls and side stepped down the stairs in the dark. Grey streaks on the plaster showed that she was not the first person to do so.

"Oh!" Tessa looked up from her laptop as if she hadn't expected to see anyone. "Good morning." She took a sip from her mug. "Did you sleep well?"

Right off, Kim sensed attitude. Just a little bit stuck up. No, as a matter of fact she slept like shit. Things in the wall—probably mice—sounded like they were building something. Tap tap, click click. Whoever slept in the bed last had left enough grit to make sandpaper, but that wasn't the worst. "There's a weird smell up there." Kim tucked in her shirt, gestured at the coffee pot.

"Please help yourself." Tessa pointed at the shelf of cups. "What kind of smell?" And then without waiting for an answer, "Cal used to keep his asparagus fertilizer under the bed but that was fifteen years ago. There's been a leak off and on depending on the ice dams but I've never heard of insulation getting moldy." Tessa squinted at her screen. "I used to dry onions on that floor but they shouldn't leave a smell." Eyes on computer screen, end of subject.

Kim dug out a packet of powdered creamer she'd taken from a Quick Stop, sprinkled it into a mug, slugged in coffee. The good thing about creamer was that it could mask the taste of day-old piss. "Let me cut to the chase." She took another sip. "Was that the room your husband died in?"

Tessa looked at Kim over the top of her glasses. "No."

Kim sipped. Not hot enough. She put her cup in the microwave and punched minute. That smell reminded her of the trailer where her grandfather died. "I'm staying put." His last words. She held his hand, touching his masonic ring. Her grandfather, the only member of her family who kept his word. I'm going to teach you to ride a bike and he did; learn to shoot a rifle and get your first deer and he did both. He'd lost his farm before she was born but he kept his tractor in half of the garage and used it to plow people's gardens, brush hog, even plow snow.

"Do you object to the smell?" Tessa widened her eyes. Even from where she stood, Kim could see smudges on her glasses. Maybe a person could ignore seeing the world through dirt but it would drive Kim crazy. So the lady lacks a filth detector and maybe a sense of smell, too.

"You're welcome to sleep in another room," Tessa said. "There's the children's alcove at the end of the hall where Laddy's old dog crate is. Or you might like the milk house. David was turning it into a library when he got sick. You could probably clear a space out there and I think there's a mattress you could bring up from—"

"No, that's okay, I'm good where I am." Kim felt tired listening to the places she could be and the stuff she would need to do if she wanted to be there.

Last night, as she lay awake with the same old problems bubbling in her cauldron of worries—where to live and what to live on—Kim got the bright idea of trading Tessa housekeeping for room and board. When she woke up she was like, *yeah!* I'm gonna clean the hell out of this place. But now, in the light of day, she was like, *whoa!* Where to start? Might have to set off a bomb.

The kitchen, the living room gave the impression of a garage sale, stuff chucked wherever. Chairs and side tables and stacks of books and toys crammed into corners and tools and magazines and boxes overflowing with recycling and a china cabinet full of rocks—rocks!—and, on top of a book case, a pyramid of collapsing pumpkins. The walls—what you could see of them—were covered with paintings, maps, posters. Notes and doodles were scribbled on the plaster. From the rafters hung bunches of herbs, dried herbs, probably years old. A wind chime made from beer tabs—kinda cool—hung motionless. Along the roof beam, a festoon of cobwebs turned gauzy in a streak of sunlight. Kim dropped her gaze to the furniture, scouting a place to sit. A brocade sofa looked in good shape but a cat slept in the center in a nest of its own fur. Meanwhile, Kim was starving.

"Mind if I have some cereal?" An open shelf held jars of *don't ask* and cans and open boxes. Mice paradise.

Tessa's glanced up. "Ah, well, let's see. There's part of a loaf of bread on the counter. We have oat groats if you want to make gruel."

"What?" Sounded like car lubricant.

"Grew-el. Hot cereal."

"Is there any Corn Flakes?" Kim squatted, peered deeper in where stuff was knocked over and a jar of something had oozed.

"No." Tessa did not look up.

"Everybody has Corn Flakes."

"Not I." Tessa tapped the keys.

Kim laughed. "Corn Flakes? Not even as a little kid?'

"Nope." Still typing.

"What was your mom, a witch?"

The conversation might have taken a darker turn had Jasper not appeared.

"Tessa's mom was a great dancer." He advanced towards Tessa swiveling his hips. "Rumba, Cha Cha."

"So she said. I never saw her so much as skip and neither did you. This is Kim." She introduced them. "She fixed the tractor."

"No shit." Jasper stared at Kim. "That's one powerful handshake. You deserve—" He looked at Tessa. "What does she deserve?"

"Corn flakes," Tessa said and Kim let out a guffaw. "I told her I've never tried them."

Jasper rolled his eyes at Kim and there passed between them a flicker of understanding that they might be comrades, based more on Jasper's ceaseless need to appeal to a new woman than on his opposition to Tessa's opinions.

"Never mind," he drawled. "You let Uncle Jasper fix you something."

Kim checked out his skinny ass in jeans and his cowboy boots. She wasn't much for the two day's whisker growth—razor burn special. She preferred red neck barbering: clean shaven or a full-on Rip Van Winkle beard.

"You don't live here, too, do you?" This guy could prove interesting.

"Not on a regular basis. I just come here as a ...", he turned mock serious—"spiritual custodian."

"I got no idea what you're talking about," Kim said.

"David was my best friend. I have concern for his widow." Jasper winked at Tessa. "Really I'm just a part time lawyer, full-time hedonist."

Kim narrowed her eyes. "Were you ever in the public defender's office?"

"Briefly."

Kim smiled. When she'd gone in to sign up for a lawyer after Bill and Melissa pressed charges, she was assigned a young guy but Jasper was on the scene and she remembered his eyebrows.

He opened a cupboard and took out what looked to Kim like an old football, sawed off two slices, dropped them in the toaster. He melted butter in a pan, cracked eggs, and scrambled them into a bowl. When had a guy ever made her breakfast? Bill sometimes brought home bagels for Christmas morning.

"I think I've seen you around town. You're from here, right?" He tilted the frying pan to spread the film of raw egg evenly.

"I used to clean for Harriet Dawson before she passed."

"Hell of a nice old lady." He gently folded the omelet back on itself and slid it onto a plate beside the toast. "Honey?" He opened a mason jar and spooned out something that looked to Kim like Bondo, slathered it on the toast.

She bit into fiberboard. Could do serious damage to her upper plate.

"You wouldn't have any Wonder Bread."

"You don't like my seven grain bread?" Tessa asked mildly.

"No, I do! I just got weak teeth." She didn't want to piss off this woman she barely knew. They might not eat the same food but they had one thing in common: they were both broke, which usually turns people against each other, at least in Kim's family. That she and Tessa weren't related might be in their favor.

"Thanks." She grinned at Jasper. "You're a good cook."

"Wait 'til you taste his baked beans." Tessa smiled.

"I'd love to," Kim said. Now was the time to nail down one edge of the flapping tarp of her life. She pulled a chair near Tessa and, keeping her voice low, asked if they could discuss her staying here. Jasper helpfully disappeared outside with his coffee.

"I don't know if you'd be open to this—" Kim paused, liking the sound of the word *open*. "—but I could trade you work around this place for room and board."

Tessa looked at her keyboard.

"I'd chip in for groceries, too. "

Silence.

"And beer. I never impose on anyone's beer."

"David was the only one who drank it," Tessa said, flatly. "And he's not here."

"And me." Jasper had drifted back into the room and was leaning against a door jam.

"I can't afford the hand-made stuff," Kim said. Jasper assured her that he wasn't picky.

Worried that she'd lost Tessa's attention, Kim explained that she was a professional and would be doing house cleaning on the side and could contribute cleaning products and stuff.

"What stuff?" Tessa asked. She went to her computer.

Was she going off on her? Maybe she shouldn't have stuck her neck out. Kim glanced at Jasper. *Help me out here.*

"Sounds like you got yourself a deal, Tess." He glanced at Kim; then his expression became serious. "This place is a big responsibility, a tremendous amount of upkeep. Too much for one person."

"Okay, Jasper, you made your point." Tessa was on the verge of tears. She felt Kim's arm circle her shoulders and she let herself sag into the warmth. "My poor husband." She sobbed. "He was blindsided."

When she was calm, she told Kim, yes, she'd be glad to have her move in for a trial period, see how things went. They could draw up a work plan. And having said this, Tessa felt as if she'd done something. She looked around her and the house clutter seemed to resolve itself into a scene that she could face, at least for the time being.

"There's just one thing," Kim said. "I have this heirloom hutch. I told my ex I'd be getting it out of his house, like, yesterday. "

"Uh huh?" Tessa stared at her computer.

"I can see you don't need another toothpick in here but I was wondering if, just temporarily—"

"Sure. There's the barn."

"It's an antique. It might get mildew."

The phone rang. Tessa grabbed the cordless, took it out on the porch.

"So—" Jasper rubbed his hands and spun around on the heel of one boot. "I take it you stayed here last night."

"Yup." Kim drank coffee.

"How do you know Tess?"

Kim was explaining that she didn't when Tessa came back with the phone.

"When it rains it pours." She smiled ruefully. "Rory has a friend who needs housing. He's bringing him over for dinner."

Best to put the hutch on hold but here was Jasper sidling over, asking how big it was and did she need a truck.

"Thanks, but give me a minute." Kim went outside. She'd kill for a cigarette, checked her pockets and came up empty. She needed to think. There were differences here. Age for one thing. Tessa was a good fifteen years older and probably set in her ways. Tessa talked like someone who'd been to college, so she had money at one time if not now, which there'd never been for Kim unless she counted the six months she shacked up with Harriet's son Jim, not that he left her any. But she didn't need college to figure out that Tessa's tractor didn't start because the air filter was dirty. The whole carburetor probably needed replacing but she wasn't getting into that until she figured out if living here was in the cards. And there was the fingernail comment. Yesterday, Tessa had looked at Kim's hands and told her that David found dirty fingernails a turn-on. Whose fingernails? Not Kim's. But she knew how weird jealousy could be. There was a time when she'd been jealous of her own underwear. She'd had to share her husband with the contents of her lingerie drawer until he moved on to plus size garter belts and open nipple bras. Now here was this lady who might be jealous of *her*, a woman her dead husband had never even met.

21

Pot Luck

Eliot stared out the window at rainy woods. He had hoped Rory and Phil would let him stay in the basement on the bed he knew they kept for house-sitters, just until he could make a plan. His other friends had been driven away by Josh's gatekeeping and he didn't feel he could impose on them. Then there were the removals. Harry and Joe, his favorite bridge partners—Josh loathed bridge—were now in Punta Cana fulltime. Once Hester's mother died, she and Kippy took over the old lady's house in Spain. They wanted visitors but Eliot couldn't afford the airfare. A group of his older friends had moved into a gay men's retirement compound on the Cape. Where was the love they had all championed? If it existed, Eliot couldn't afford a piece of it.

He hadn't cared about money or he would have majored in something more lucrative than history. For decades he'd been the day editor of the North Haven Monitor, nicknamed the

Monster, a job he'd loved until the paper, near bankruptcy, was bought by a media chain that paid reporters less than minimum wage. Josh had been a commerce major until he realized he hated math. Nonetheless, he worked as a bank teller until they met and he moved to North Haven, found work in a frame shop and began trading antiques on the side. Every weekend at dawn they went hunting and gathering down back roads wherever a pink tag sale sign pointed. After they'd hit the flea markets, they picnicked by brooks. Now that earlier life seemed a dream.

Rory pulled into Tessa's dooryard, lamenting the mud that spattered on his freshly washed car. Eliot had noticed that his friend seemed more adapted to urban than rural life, not that Eliot should judge. He and Josh had spent their lives in town.

"I think you and Tess will get along very well." Rory led Eliot up the garden path. "You both love flowers."

"What flowers?" Eliot glanced at Japanese knotweed and golden rod.

"Be reasonable!" Rory sidestepped a muddy toy truck, its wheels missing as if cannibalized by elves. "It's been a hard year for her, as I told you. She's let a few things slide." He made his way slowly. "You don't mind that I'm re-gifting your wine. You could say it's from you."

Eliot tripped over a broken flagstone and Rory lunged for his arm.

"Careful now, we don't want any more fractures."

Phil was at home with his foot up.

Eliot pulled his arm away.

"Listen my dear boy, I'm trying to help you." Rory took his arm. "Do not look a gift horse."

"I see only black everywhere. Oceans of black." He dropped a jumbo bag of corn chips in the mud, picked it up. "How could I have abandoned my life. I must be mad."

"You aren't mad, but Josh was." Rory said. "But if you really feel that way, Tessa's house will help you recover."

They reached a grimy glass door. Eliot thought he glimpsed, somewhere within, the sparkle of fairy lights.

"If you take the wine—", Rory handed Eliot the bottle—"I'll just—" Rory gripped the edge of the slider with both hands and, with a grunt, hoisted it upward, forcing it back on its track. "And I'll—" He leaned against the glass, pushing. "Just ... get ... this ...open." When the door was wide enough, Rory slid inside. Then Eliot turned sideways and squeezed through the opening.

"Well!" he gasped. In the gloom, he bumped into some kind of iron mechanism. "I guess this repels intruders. Jesus, where are we?" Newspapers and bulging garbage bags were stacked to the ceiling.

"Come ahead!" a woman's voice called from inside. "I haven't finished picking up from the funeral."

"Dear God, that was four months ago." Rory pushed aside a humidifier, a commode and a guitar case. "Just follow me, darling."

Eliot got his pant leg snagged on the edge of a defunct wood stove.

"You've seen the worst," Rory said. "This is the mud room, a New England tradition."

"I see mud," Eliot muttered. "But not a room."

Somewhere a dog growled. The growling came closer.

"I don't do dogs," Eliot whimpered. "They hate me."

"Tessa doesn't keep animals, I can assure you." Rory again took his friend's arm.

"Satan!" A man's voice "*Get* over here!"

"Jasper, is that you?" Rory called. He moved milk crates of cassette tapes and CDs. "Do you have a canine with you and is it under control? Otherwise, my friend cannot come further."

"Do not say that!" Eliot hissed. "Makes me sound hysterical."

"Well, aren't you?" Rory widened his eyes.

"It's okay!" Jasper yelled. "He's in a crate."

They opened a door onto murk and weak glimmers of lamplight. Eliot took a deep breath and began coughing. When he'd recovered, he stood breathing shallowly, taking in a scene that reminded him of the night bazaar he and Josh had visited in Sharm el Sheik. Inside narrow shops, the atmosphere was thick with the smoke of charcoal braziers. Dim electric bulbs reflected a trove of copper and brass and colored glass. Men in dark robes sat close together drinking tea and passing hookahs. Eliot had imagined himself escaping from Josh and disappearing into the thronged passageways of the souk.

Something was on fire. Under a hanging lamp, a woman bent over a smoking oven. A man in cowboy boots and tight jeans handed her a big box of salt and she dumped the contents into the oven, dousing the fire. An atmosphere of exotic clutter surrounded them. Shelves held oddly shaped pottery, or possibly gourds. Implements dangled. Topaz ribbons hung from the rafters and caught the light in momentary sparkles.

"Better than a fire extinguisher," she said, turning, and Eliot knew he'd seen her before. "Ah!" She put down the salt box and approached, arms held in front of her, hands dangling as though they were newly acquired and she was just learning their use. "Eliot! We met once long ago." She shook his hand and Eliot was surprised to feel stubby, warm fingers. "I'm so sorry," she came close. "About your loss. We'll talk later." He gave her the bag of corn chips.

"This is *perfect!*", she cried to the room in general. "The sweet potatoes exploded, but you've brought a replacement," She held up the chip bag. "Jasper made his baked beans, so now we have a complete protein."

"How you doing, man?" Jasper gripped Eliot's hand, then turned to Rory. "Awesome sweater, man."

"You don't think it makes me look fat?" Rory gestured at himself.

Jasper turned back to Eliot. "Rory's keeping Dubreault's Menswear alive. Main Street is going down, man, going down. Economic end times. The panhandlers are hitting up each other."

Eliot listened in a daze. This was North Haven, his hometown where he'd once owned a shop, but been he'd out of the business gossip loop since Josh got sick; he'd lost track.

"Yo! *Jasper!*" A woman's voice came from the cellar. "Don't leave me holding this thing."

"Oops." Jasper nodded to Rory and Eliot and disappeared into another room.

While Rory uncorked the wine and found glasses, Tessa wrestled with a cabbage that escaped her knife and rolled off the cutting board and the counter. Rory retrieved it and attempted to brush off the dust and crumbs it had acquired in its trip across the floor.

Tessa rooted in the depths of a cupboard. "The good knife lost its handle but there's this." She brought out a machete.

"Jesus, no!" Eliot stepped back.

"Where did *that* come from?" Rory exclaimed. "Stay away from that thing."

"Oh, for crying out loud." Tessa positioned the blade on top of the cabbage and bore down, splitting it in half.

"Goodness." Eliot stared at the unpolished steel blade, the rough wooden handle. "How did that get here?"

"No idea." She quartered the cabbage, wiped the blade. "Things have a way of accumulating here. Rory might remember."

"That might have been Timmy's," Rory said. "Jasper's friend who went to Cuba, remember him?"

"Oh yes, the one who began the tree house. Jasper!" she called. "What happened to Timmy?"

Around the corner came Jasper, walking backward and holding one end of a long grey cupboard.

"You talking to me?" He was breathing hard as he edged into the kitchen. "I heard he's in Alaska but that was years ago. Christ, this thing weighs. Must be lined with lead."

Kim came into view carrying the other end. "Those beers might not have been wise." Sweat shone on her forehead.

Tessa glanced around from where she was grating cabbage. "I thought we decided on the barn."

Jasper put his end down and flexed his hands. "You been out there lately?"

"Of course I've been out there," Tessa said.

"Then you know there's not much roof left." Jasper glanced at Kim.

"Like twenty percent," Kim added.

Tessa considered this assessment of the roof. "That should be some protection," she said. "Or you can cover it with a tarp and take it back to the cellar."

Kim looked at Tessa through her eyebrows. "Cellar floor is pretty swampy." They'd tracked mud through the kitchen that was even then becoming part of the general filth. "We only came that way because no other door was wide enough." She needed to be polite but she also wanted to protect her one valuable.

"Well, it can't stay in the middle of the kitchen," Rory said.

"No kidding." Kim laughed.

"Well!" Tessa exclaimed brightly. "Rory, would you find a place for it while I finish making dinner?" Eliot watched as she pulled down a grater from a hook. Her expression remained impassive as she lined up the cabbage chunks with her oddly shaped fingers and set to work. This was a woman who had dealt with considerably more difficult situations than placing a piece of unwanted furniture.

"It will be perfectly fine in the annex."

"Satan's out there in the crate," Jasper said. "I don't want to stir him up."

Rory looked at him in annoyance. "Why on earth would you bring that animal over here? You know she hates dogs." Tessa ignored this comment.

"He seized on the way home from the vet and I didn't want him to be alone. Give me a second." He renewed his grip on the cupboard. Kim pivoted her end around the counter and they began inching it into the living room.

Eliot stood with a glass of wine watching the placement of the hutch. In all his days at flea markets, rarely had he encountered a more hideous piece of furniture. A useless object cobbled together of barn boards, probably by a fraternity boy furnishing his boom boom room. He looked around for the wine and was relieved to see Rory scavenging the cupboards for more.

"Just for now, why don't we double park it," Jasper suggested. He and Kim had trundled the cupboard to a spot in front of an upright piano.

"The piano's missing too many keys anyway." Once the object had taken its place in the hodgepodge, Tessa seemed to lose interest while Kim unpacked votive candles and snifters and arranged them on the shelves. She stood back to admire.

"So you inherited this piece?" Fortified with wine from David's liquor cabinet, Eliot felt perversely interested in the object he had just condemned. Its owner made an unusual addition to this little group with her masses of red curls, her broad shoulders and foghorn voice.

Kim was explaining the hutch's provenance and the stature of her grandfather when Tessa announced dinner.

Eliot and Kim moved to the table while Tessa served from the far end. She had resurrected the sweet potatoes, mashed and topped with cheese. Jasper's baked beans steamed in an earthenware pot beside a bowl of coleslaw. Rory found a big mixing bowl for the corn chips. As she filled plates, Tessa talked about the joys of the day.

"I love to watch the clouds overspreading the sky. Such a relief after all that blue."

"I adore the sun," said Rory.

"But don't you find it can be oppressive? Rain and clouds lower my stress level."

Rory said that a cloudy day made him anxious. Jasper said that this rain was just a passing front, not enough to affect the water table after such a dry summer.

Eliot did not offer an opinion but thought, privately, that he might stick with red wine and corn chips. He watched Kim go to work on her platter. She and Jasper were drinking beer.

"So I take it you live here," Eliot said. "Or your furniture does."

"I just got here yesterday," Kim said, her mouth full. "I'm. ...sort of...like..."

"In transition?"

"I guess you might say that." She swallowed, lowered her voice. "My ex and my daughter kicked me out of the house."

"Oh my God." Eliot leaned closer. "I'm sorry."

"Well actually I had it coming."

Eliot widened his eyes.

"I pulled a gun on them." Kim whispered, then chuckled. "Not the smartest move."

Eliot looked around. Their hostess and Rory were deep in conversation about her new song lyrics and Jasper had gotten up for more beer.

"Does Tessa know?" he whispered.

"We didn't get to that." Kim forked up coleslaw. "My family didn't tell the cops so I got charged with simple assault, which I have to say I really appreciate. I did anger management, just finished parole."

"Oh, good." Eliot wasn't sure where to take the conversation when Kim continued.

"I can see if it had just been my ex, but when your own daughter calls the cops on you—" She stared at her plate. "It stings."

"I can imagine." Although he couldn't. Josh's act wasn't a threat, it was the goal.

While Kim got a beer, Eliot sipped wine and observed the room. A more chaotic mess he had rarely seen. Tessa seemed relaxed, in her element, as she sang softly,

" '—*waylaid by your style/ swindled by your smile*—' is that too much alliteration?"

"Mm," Rory considered. "I wonder about 'swindled.' Do you really want to say he defrauded you?"

"So." Kim sat down again. "I hear you're moving in."

"Well," Eliot swallowed a mouthful of chips. "Tentatively."

"Are you new around here?" She took a slug of beer.

"No. We're, I—" He paused, mind spinning. "My husband just killed himself, and I'm bankrupt and homeless."

Kim gaped. "Good Lord, is the devil chasing you!"

Eliot laughed weakly. "He caught up."

"I need a cigarette," Kim said.

Eliot excused himself and followed Kim outside. Jasper joined them.

"I don't really smoke," Eliot splashed breathlessly through weeds to the disused front door and its sheltering roof.

* * *

"So, what's the verdict on Eliot?" Rory asked Tessa.

"I've no idea, haven't talked to him." She examined a broken thumbnail. "He and Kim seem to be compatible."

"Kim." Rory looked around to be sure they were alone. "Now that one is a piece of work. She used to clean for friends of ours until she got arrested. "

"Oh, no. For what?"

"No idea but it must have been in the paper. Oh, that's right, we don't have a paper any more."

Tessa sighed. "A felon in our midst."

"No, no, no!" Rory tried to reassure her. "Maybe just a D.U.I. That's not a felony is it? Jasper would know, and look how chummy the two of *them* are."

"I'll have to have a word with him."

Kim held out her cigarette.

"I might as well tell you what I just told her." Eliot accepted the cigarette and turned to Jasper. "Everyone's bound to find out." He described his recent catastrophe.

"Christ on a stick, man, I am so sorry." Jasper put his hand on Eliot's shoulder.

"Shock is weird," Eliot took a drag, coughed. He returned the cigarette. "Sometimes I feel almost giddy." He wiped his eyes. "Being here— I feel like I've escaped into another life. And Tessa's so welcoming, so tolerant—"

"Until she's not," Jasper said

"Like how?" Kim asked.

"I can't explain," Jasper said. "You'll see."

They were silent, listening to rain, the cinders of two cigarettes glowing between cupped fingers.

"Do you think he's a predator?" Rory sat closer. "When I see him downtown, he always looks like he's on the hunt."

"A womanizer but not predator." Tessa stared at her computer.

"What's the diff?"

"Oh, for crying out loud!" Tessa exclaimed. "Jasper's not psycho if that's what you mean."

When Rory didn't reply she felt called on to keep defending her husband's friend.

"He's a bit flaky but he's been wonderful to me. He's employed, he has a house, or he did."

"And he is not going to live here," Rory said.

"Why do you care?"

"There's something sleazy about him," Rory said. "It's just a feeling."

"Rory, you're not being helpful." Tessa glared. "David could be very sleazy, as you well know."

"No, this is a different sleazy."

"I don't want to lead the jury about Tess. She's a great woman," Jasper said. "We all live in our own worlds, like what you were saying about running away to a different life." He directed this to Eliot. "That's a survival strategy."

"If you have a car and gas," said Kim.

"What does this have to do with Tessa?" Eliot asked.

"Just that she's an escape artist." Jasper blew a smoke ring and watched it disappear in the rain.

"Just meeting her, she seems so relaxed, so grounded," Eliot said. "And she's lived here for decades."

Jasper tapped his temple. "I'm talking about what happens inside."

"And I'm not." Eliot was suddenly assertive. "I'm just trying to get through the day."

"I can relate to that." Kim stubbed out her cigarette and pocketed it. "My feet are wicked wet and I'm going inside."

* * *

"I'm looking for people who can function," Tessa said. "Pay me some rent and not make trouble."

"Function?" Rory asked.

"Stop playing." Tessa glared at her friend. "Someone who can get up in the morning and help out around here, then go out and be part of the cash economy. No addicts or clinically insane. I'm not running a halfway house."

"Hi!" Rory looked over her head. "Pretty wet out there, eh?"

"You got that right." Kim scuffed out of her shoes, peeled off her socks. "I'm going to the washroom if that's okay."

"Of course!" Tessa said. When Kim had disappeared, she resumed at a whisper. "You said Eliot was practically catatonic."

"Oh, that was a few days ago. He seems fine now," Rory said. "He needs a goddamn job is what he needs, but I'm not sure how employable he is. Oh, there you are!" He greeted Eliot. "I was just telling Tessa that you're job hunting."

Tessa asked what he hoped to do.

"Oh—" Eliot yearned to go to sleep. "Something unskilled until I figure out where my skills went."

"Of *course* you have skills!" Rory shouted. "You're an investigative journalist and a framer of artworks. You were a shopowner, so you're skilled at business principles."

"Actually Josh kept the books."

" And you're an antiquarian." Rory smiled triumphantly at this catalogue of his friend's achievements.

Eliot could say nothing. He felt demoralized by Rory's inflated description.

Kim returned pulling up her fly. "You're gonna need a new ballcock."

"I beg your pardon?" Rory feigned horror.

"Did you jiggle it?" Tessa asked.

"Ouch!" Rory shrieked. "That's what he said!"

Jasper appeared in the annex door. "I'm shoving off. Satan needs to go home." An elderly black lab followed slowly on a leash.

Eliot looked pleadingly at his friend and Rory agreed that they, too should leave. Perhaps Eliot could come over in the morning with his things? Tessa agreed.

As they drove down the unlighted woods road, Eliot felt what was left of his good mood drowned out by the hum of anxiety. He was a refugee from his former life and tomorrow he'd move in with virtual strangers and do what he did not know.

Sensing his agitation, Rory talked about how fortunate they were to know someone with spare rooms and how compatible he and Tessa would be, especially after he'd had good night's sleep. "And think how much better it is to be here than in that rat infested Candlestick."

Eliot had to admit that Tessa's seemed friendlier than the Stick, if not cleaner.

Kim stubbed out her nightcap cigarette and felt her way upstairs in the dark. She was grateful to Jasper for fronting her half of his cigarette pack and buying a six pack, even more for helping her with the hutch. What he meant about Tessa she had no idea. Some guys liked to pretend they knew more than anyone else when all they were doing was messing with your head. But she felt good moving the hutch with him. It'd been a long time since she had anyone she liked to work with. Of course, he had a job when he wanted to do it. That Eliot she didn't expect to last long around here. His being gay didn't bother her – it was his personality, if he even had one, which she couldn't tell.

No point in keeping herself awake. She'd got herself the basics. Tomorrow she'd do some sweeping, some recreational floor washing. See how that worked out. She'd left her cleaning caddy at Bill's. Maybe Melissa would drop it off, visit her mom's new place which, Kim had to admit, wasn't half bad. She'd lived in worse and liked it.

Photo By Laura Moscowitz

Mimi Morton wrote fiction and freelance journalism before and after retiring from her career teaching English and Humanities at Dawson College in Montréal and at Keene State College in New Hampshire. Her fiction appeared in several small New England literary magazines. She wrote freelance for newspapers in the U.S. and Canada, and gave commentary on CBC radio. Shortly before she died in 2021, she published a memoir, *Before the Age of Reason*. Mimi excelled as a gardener, bird-watcher, naturalist, and as a great cook. She lived in southern Vermont with her husband.

www.ingramcontent.com/pod-product-compliance
Lightning Source LLC
LaVergne TN
LVHW040045080526
838202LV00045B/3503